PREACH NO MORE

RECENT MYSTERIES BY RICHARD LOCKRIDGE

Murder in False Face
Troubled Journey
Twice Retired

WITH FRANCIS LOCKRIDGE

Murder by the Book
Quest of the Bogeyman

AS FRANCIS RICHARDS

With Option to Die
A Plate of Red Herrings
Die Laughing
A Risky Way to Kill

Richard Lockridge

PREACH NO MORE

BOOK CLUB ASSOCIATES
LONDON

This edition published 1972 by
Book Club Associates
by arrangement with Hutchinson Publishing Group Ltd.

Printed in Great Britain
by The Anchor Press Ltd.,
and bound by Wm. Brendon & Son Ltd.,
both of Tiptree, Essex

1

It was Rachel Farmer's idea, and Anthony Cook responded to it with no enthusiasm. His response was, "For God's sake, why?"

He had been on the four-to-midnight shift and it is a shift which inhibits. Lunch had now and then been possible, but lunch is not really a substitute. And painters, for the most part, work by daylight, so that Rachel, at hours suitable for lunch, was too often standing on a low platform in an underheated studio and trying not to shiver. Most of the painters for whom she posed grew fretful if she, to any noticeable degree, shivered. They were inclined to say, "Damn it, girl, stay *still!* Freeze it the way I showed you."

"And 'freeze' is the word for it, mister," Rachel Farmer now and then told Tony Cook. "Because mostly I don't have anything on, and studios are like barns. And skylights leak air. And in the end it doesn't look like me anyway. It's better with photographers, because with them I wear clothes. Only then it's those damn lights."

Tony Cook had seen one or two of the paintings for which Rachel had posed and realized that they didn't, on the whole, look like her. He thought this a pity—thought it a waste of long, delicately rounded grace. He had at first assumed it was because the men she modeled for could not draw. She had corrected him. It was not that they could not draw, she explained. It was that they had gone beyond drawing. "Drawing," she explained, "is for illustrators. And that's a dirty word."

It was a Wednesday evening in late March when Rachel had her idea. It was, as late March evenings go in Manhattan, a rather pleasant one. It had been a short walk from his new apartment to the apartment in Gay Street. It was much better to walk a few blocks than to take the long subway ride down from the West Bronx. From the new apartment he could walk to Gay Street and, in only a few more minutes, to West Twentieth Street. It worked out very well, especially when the walk was to Gay Street.

He climbed the one flight to Rachel's apartment in the short and crooked street and, outside her door, looked at his watch. It was six-thirty, which was the time appointed. He pressed a button and there were chimes inside, and the shield over the peephole in the door popped open and she looked out at him, using one brown eye. It was a large brown eye.

"I'm not quite dressed," she said through the peephole. "But hi, Tony." The knob grated and the door partly opened, and he pushed it the rest of the way.

"You're sure not quite dressed," he said, as he watched her walk across the living room away from him toward the bedroom.

She was not dressed at all.

She turned and smiled at him, and he thought for the several hundredth time, My God, have I got me something!

"Oh," Rachel said, "except for clothes. My face is all on."

She went on into the bedroom, long and slim and naked. He was about to tell her she needn't bother; that she was fine as she was; that she was lovely as she was. But she closed the bedroom door, and he took his jacket off and unstrapped shoulder holster and gun and put his jacket on again and measured bourbon onto ice in a glass and went to the refrigerator, where La Ina and a glass for it were chilling. He did not pour La Ina into the sherry glass because, poured, it would lose its chill. He did not drink from his own glass but merely stood in the living room and looked at the closed bedroom door. It was fine to have an evening again.

She was not long. It never took her long to dress when she thought of dressing. She came out of the bedroom in a pale yellow suit, with a white blouse under the jacket, and he thought, My God, have I got me something, and said, "Hi, lady," and poured chilled sherry into the chilled glass. They carried their drinks to a sofa and sat side by side. They clicked glasses. They did not kiss. When they kissed it was not casually, between sips. A kiss was a beginning, not a token.

"I want to go to the Garden," Rachel Farmer said. "I want to hear this Prentis man."

It was then that Tony Cook said, "For God's sake, why?"

She looked at him with what appeared to be surprise.

"Why," she said, "I never have. And somebody told me I mustn't miss him. And this is the last night he'll be there. From here he goes on to save Chicago, and I don't much like Chicago."

"You don't need saving," Tony told her. He was firm about it. "You wouldn't really like being saved."

"Oh, it isn't personal," Rachel said. She sipped her sherry. "It's just that I never saw one. Not Billy Sunday or anybody."

"Billy Sunday," Tony said and took a rather large swallow of his drink. "Billy Sunday died years before you were born. Billy Graham?"

"Clean-cut," Rachel said. "And palsy with Nixon." She spoke with finality.

"Look," he said. "The thing starts at eight or thereabouts. I thought a couple of drinks and then maybe Charles. Or uptown some place, if you'd rather."

"Charles Restaurant isn't going to Chicago," she said. "We can grab a hamburger."

"Well," Tony said. "It wasn't precisely what I had in mind."

When she is amused, Rachel Farmer's smile is wide. It was wide then.

"Mister," she said. "I know what you had in mind. Or, I guess I do. We'll go and be saved and then come back here and you can show me if I guessed right."

She raised her eyebrows. He looked at her for several moments. Then he smiled back at her. His smile was not as wide as hers, but it was what smile he had.

"All right," he said. "It's a crazy way to spend an evening, but all right."

He finished his drink. For a moment he looked at the long slim legs below the short suit-skirt. He sighed. He went to the table which was the bar and poured himself another drink. He carried the sherry bottle back with him and poured into her glass. After a time he buckled his gun on again, and they walked the few blocks to Eighth and Sixth and sat on stools and ate hamburgers. His was too well done.

Madison Square Garden once was near Manhattan's Madison Square, but that was many years ago. It moved far uptown on Eighth Avenue; it came downtown again and replaced a gracious railroad station as part of a structure which towers above Seventh Avenue and is without any special grace.

"I used to love Penn Station," Rachel said. "When I was young, I used to go there and think about trains. There wasn't a train I wouldn't have taken, no matter where it was going. That's Millay, sort of. There isn't any more station and there aren't any more trains."

"It's still a station," Tony said. "There are still trains."

"Not real trains," she said. "I rode the Century once. It was a fine train." She was on the curb side and slid out of the low, tight cab. "Even if it did go to Chicago," she said and waited while he paid and struggled out of the cab. He said, "And taxis used to be built for people," and they went into the entrance of Madison Square Garden. They went on elevators and up ramps. They passed ticket windows and all were closed, and over each there was a sign which read "Salvation Is Without Price." They went up further ramps and into a vast and dimly lighted hall. It was almost filled with people who rustled in their seats.

Organ music swelled through the enormous space. "Bach," Rachel said, and they found seats. Anthony Cook made sure they were close to an exit ramp.

At the far end of the amphitheater, a platform cut across the hall. It was draped in white. Centered in the rear of the platform there was a towering cross. There was nobody on the platform, but it was from that end of the hall that the organ music swelled. Then the music surged and the hall seemed to shake with it, and then the music stopped. For a minute or more, the crowd—must be thousands, Tony thought—rustled in the quiet. Here and there somebody coughed.

Then light slowly built on the stage, coming down on it from above. As the light grew, organ music began again. I ought to know that one, Tony thought, and Rachel said "Onward, Christian Soldiers," her voice low. The sound of the organ lessened after a moment, and then singing began and, from the right of the platform, a choir of men and women marched to the beat of the hymn—marched in a double line. All were in white robes. A tall man, robed like the others, led the marchers and led in the singing. "Marching as to war, With the cross of Jesus Going on before."

The double line stretched across the platform, in front of the towering cross. They stopped and turned and faced the audience, and the leader stood in front of them, also facing forward. Then a spotlight leaped down on him, and he turned and faced the double line of choir. There was a silver cross on the back of his robe. He raised his hands toward the choir, and the organ stopped for a moment and then began again.

It played softly and the voices of the choir rose over it, surging through the hall. "A mighty fortress is our God."

"They're good, aren't they?" Rachel whispered. "They're very good."

Tony Cook nodded his head. They were good, all right. There must be a hundred of them, he thought. It's quite a production, he thought. All right, it's one hell of a production. Most of the members of the choir are young, he thought. The women have young faces. It is hard to tell when they are so far away, but some of the faces seem to be pretty faces.

"A girl I know is in there somewhere," Rachel said. "It's too far away to tell which she is." A gray-haired woman in the seat next Rachel's said, "Shhh!" But Rachel's voice had been very low, so low that Tony could hardly hear her. "She sings in nightclubs when she can get jobs," Rachel said, her voice so softly low that he had to lean toward her to hear.

"This is the house of God," the gray-haired woman said, her voice louder than Rachel's and most stern.

"I'm sorry," Rachel said, and they listened, with the rest of the hushed thousands, to the singing of the hymn. The hymn ended and the lights dimmed on the stage. When light came up again the choir singers were divided, half on either side of the stage. When the lights came up they shone on the great white cross. The choir leader stood in front of it. He came forward, almost to the edge of the platform and the organ began again.

"Rock of ages, cleft for me," the leader sang. His voice was baritone. It sounded to Tony Cook like a fine voice. He looked at Rachel and she nodded her head. She leaned toward him and whispered. "He was in grand opera a few years ago," she whispered. "That's what my friend tells me, anyway. He—"

"Shhh!"

The singer was a tall man with the spotlights shining on him, glancing from his white robe. Presence, Tony thought. That's what he's got. Along with a voice. No mike, either. But there's amplification somewhere. There has to be. Above him somewhere, in the shadows, there's a mike.

The singer finished "Rock of Ages." The lights dimmed again. Four Negro men in white robes, their faces startlingly dark above the whiteness, came from the right of the stage and the organ began again. "The old-time religion," the quartet sang, spotlights playing on them. "It was good for Paul and Silas and it's good enough for me." There was beat in their singing. It was almost the beat of jazz. They finished that. They sang a spiritual, their voices softer, caressing. When they had finished it they parted, and two went to the right and two to the left, and they stood in front of the choir lines. The music followed them. Then it dimmed out and, with it, the lights dimmed again. When they came up they were again on the tall cross.

The cross began slowly to rise into the air, the lights following it upward. As it rose, it exposed a white wall. A man in black stood in front of the wall and, when the cross was high above him, the lights dropped to the man. He moved forward, slowly, under the lights.

He was tall and black-haired. He wore a black suit and a clerical collar. As he walked forward, his hands—long hands, white in the light from the spot—were clasped against his chest.

He stopped near the edge of the stage and for a moment merely stood. Then he raised his arms, reaching out as if in benediction. He still did not speak. He waited, as if for silence. But the crowd was hushed in a kind of rapt intensity. He better be good, Tony Cook thought. With this buildup, he'd better be damn good.

"I come as the voice of one crying in the wilderness," the

man said. He did not speak loudly, but his voice filled the auditorium. It was a deep voice, and silk threads seemed to run through it. Tony felt a shiver go through his mind. Perhaps it went through his body. And from the audience there was a faintly sibilant sound which was very like a sigh—a sigh of contentment, of relaxation.

"The wilderness is yours," the man said, his voice still low. "It is the wilderness of your city. O your wicked city. I come to reason with you. To caution you. Only through our Lord Jesus Christ can you—you of this city—find salvation. Let me show you the wickedness you—for all of you are guilty—have let engulf the city of New York."

He moved a little to his left, the light moving with him. Then he turned, so that he stood in profile, and raised his right hand and pointed toward the white wall.

The lights dimmed, except for the spotlight which still beat down on the man in black, and there was a picture on the white wall, which had become a motion-picture screen. But there was no path of flickering light to the screen. Of course, Tony thought. Projecting from behind, through the screen.

There was a picture of the New York skyline, and the camera had swept across it, slowly, pausing now and then to peer at the city's towers. No sound came from the screen.

"A city of beauty," the man in black said. "A city of beauty and of evil. Look upon the evil of your city."

The towers of the city vanished from the screen. A street, crowded with traffic and with people, came onto the screen and grew closer as the camera zeroed toward it. The street, to Tony, became familiar. It was Forty-second Street; the block of Forty-second west of Times Square.

The camera moved from side to side of the street. It stopped to stare at the front of a movie theater; to linger on the marquee sign. "Now Showing," the sign read, "Strange Wedding." The words, "Nakedest Show in Town," followed the picture's title and there were quotation marks around the words, although the comment was not ascribed to anybody.

The camera dropped to the theater's entrance, which was partly blocked by a framed poster on which the picture's title was repeated and on which, also, there was a photograph of a woman who was, certainly, naked but had been photographed turned away from the camera. She faced into the lobby of the little theater, and the impression intended, Tony Cook thought, was that if one followed the direction her breasts pointed in, she would probably turn around.

The picture on the screen moved down Forty-second Street. It peered at other theaters. It peered into the windows of bookshops. In one window it lingered on a book called *The Human Form*, which had, on its cover, a painting of a naked couple locked in each other's arms. Or perhaps, Tony thought, it was a photograph, not a painting. Under the book was a sign which read: "In full color."

There were other books in other windows, and the camera closed on them and lingered. *Strange Practices*, one of the books was titled. On another, there were the words, *Torture Through the Ages*, and the lettering was in red and seemed to be dripping blood.

The camera moved along the street, from shop to shop. Over one shop there was a sign which read, "Devices Unlimited." Another shop offered "Novelties for All." A movie was showing a picture called *Kong's Queen*, and the poster the camera had centered on pictured a naked girl being, apparently, carried away by an outsized ape.

The camera picked up people—picked up a somewhat too rounded girl in a skirt which reached a little below her hips and whose buttocks swayed alarmingly. As she passed men she looked up at them, her whole body a question and an offer. The camera picked up two men—also walking away from it—and one of the men had his long hair caught with a ribbon at the back. He minced.

The man in black did not comment on the picture. He merely stood, his arm raised and pointing.

He's made his point, Tony thought. It's a bad block. The block beyond it's bad too. We know it's bad. This was shot in the daytime, and it's worse in the evenings and at night. So, he's made his point. He's—

The picture ended, after a brief concentration on a drunk asleep, his back against a building.

The man in black walked back to the center of the stage and the light beat down on him.

"This is your city," he said, after a moment of standing with his hands stretched out toward the audience. "This sinful city is your city. You have let it become a sink of iniquity. Because you have not followed in the footsteps of our Lord Jesus Christ. I come to you to caution and beseech. Turn to Christ. Together, with His guidance, you can cleanse this city. And through His grace—only through His grace—each of you can find salvation."

It's the voice that does it, Tony thought, after some ten minutes of listening. The voice is a wonderful voice. He's not saying what has not been said before; isn't, I suppose, said every Sunday from pulpits across the country. We are all sinners before the Lord, in whom lies our redemption. It's his voice which sends shivers. It's the whole production.

Sure, New York is a sinful city. All cities are sinful cities and always have been. And probably always will be. More open about it now, is all.

He was, he found, listening with only a part of his mind. "Afraid to walk the streets at night. Because we have forgotten God."

And because people are jammed together more tightly, Tony thought. And because they don't accept that as inevitable any more. And because the whole structure of society is changing and isn't changing fast enough for some and is changing too fast for others. And because people can come to this sinful city and get almost enough to live on when they can't get jobs, instead of staying where they were born and starving quietly. And because—

"Make your decision for Christ," the man in black said, in a voice Tony Cook thought he probably would never forget. "Accept the mercy, the infinite compassion, of the Lord. Only through—"

There are very few Negroes here, Tony thought, looking around at the audience. He could see chiefly the backs of heads because he had chosen seats strategically near an exit ramp. Very few of them were the backs of Negro heads. Few of them were the backs of young heads. They have heard all this before, Tony thought. They have come because of the voice. Because it's one hell of a good show and no admission charged. But it must cost a hell of a lot of money.

Tony was conscious that the voice had stopped and that people in the audience had begun to cough. He stopped looking at the back of heads and looked again at the stage. The organ had begun again, and the choir, still lined on either side of the platform, had begun again to sing. "Jesus loves me, this I know, for the Bible tells me so." They sang very softly.

The tall man had disappeared. His place had been taken by a much smaller man, also in clericals. He held a hand mike and spoke into it, and his voice was harsh.

"The voice will be heard again," the small man said. "Now an opportunity will be given you, you of the faithful gathered in your thousands to hear the word of God, to help make possible the carrying on of our work. Disciples will pass among you. Give with the generosity of your hearts. Salvation is at stake."

The choir continued to sing. Men and women, white-robed, moved in aisles, came up ramps. The lights in the auditorium were up.

The collectors carried cans, with slots in the tops. On the cans, which were passed down the rows from hand to hand, were the words: "Give for Salvation." Tony folded a dollar bill and slipped it through the slot and reached the can across Rachel to the woman beyond her—the woman who had *shh*ed. So far as Tony could see, the woman did not put anything into the can. Which was none of his business.

"When he comes back again," Rachel said, "it's the big moment. Anyway, my friend says it is. The one who's in the choir."

He said, "Yes?"

"It's the come-to-Jesus part," Rachel said. "Janet says it's very impressive. They go up the aisles to be saved. Sometimes more than a hundred, she says. But there's one man—she knows because he limps, and when they're being saved the choir doesn't usually really sing, and she can watch—comes up every night to be saved. Has been doing it every night for the last six weeks. Not every night, of course, because the Rangers have home games. And there's another with a white beard, and he wears sandals and—"

The woman next her said, "Shhh!" But all around people were getting their coughing done, and the choir was singing very softly from very far away. It was singing, "Lead, kindly Light, amid the encircling gloom."

Tony Cook said, "Hmmm." He said, "Do you want to stay and be impressed?"

"I don't think so," Rachel said. "I thought—oh, I guess, that it would be livelier. It's—sedate, isn't it?"

The woman said, "Shhh!" and turned and looked at Rachel. Her look was baleful. "His is the voice of God, young woman."

"I'm sure," Tony said, and stood up and reached his hand down to Rachel, who took it and stood with him. "He's in very good voice tonight," Tony said, and, still hand in hand, they went down the ramp. After a few steps, Rachel said, "Probably this is sacrilege," and they parted hands.

They got a cab in Seventh Avenue and, since there is little point in giving a hacker an address in Gay Street, Tony said, "Sixth Avenue and Waverly Place." The driver said, "That's down near Washington Square, mister?" Tony promised to guide him.

"A return to fundamentals," Rachel said. "I read some place that Billy Graham has entertainers. People like Ethel Waters. This—this was just like church. But he has a beautiful voice. Do you believe in God, Tony?"

"I don't know," Tony said. "Sometimes, I guess. But not very much, I guess. Not since I went to Sunday School. This will do, driver."

They walked from Sixth Avenue through Waverly Place and into Gay Street, and around the crook in Gay Street and up a flight of stairs.

In the apartment she sat on the sofa and nudged her shoes off. She said, to the tall man standing and looking down at her, "You can take your gun off, mister."

He took his jacket off and unstrapped his shoulder holster. When he turned back from putting it on top of the book case, she had taken off her suit jacket. He reached both hands down to her, and she took his hand and came up into his arms.

"So this is what you had in mind," she said, when her lips were hers to use. "Carnal sin. That's what you had in mind all the time, mister. The blouse has a zipper. Sometimes it sticks."

The zipper did not stick.

"Carnal sin, undoubtedly," Rachel said when later they lay relaxed. "And very nice, too."

2

A bell jangled Cook out of sleep. It still was dark in his small apartment in West Twelfth Street—an apartment which was costing him a lot more than he could afford; an apartment in which he still bumped into things in the dark. He looked at his watch, and the illuminated dial blurred to sleepy eyes. It seemed to be six o'clock. The alarm was set for seven, and something had gone wrong with—

The bell kept on jangling and jangled in spurts. Tony reached toward the telephone by his bed and banged his hand against the table it stood on. Things still weren't in the right places. He found the telephone and said, "Homicide, Detective Cook," because the sleep fuzz was still in his mind. A voice said, "Shapiro, Tony," and Tony Cook came awake. He said, "Morning, Lieutenant."

"Down in your part of town," Lieutenant Nathan Shapiro told Detective (1st gr.) Anthony Cook. "Place called the Village Brawl. Something like that. Know it?"

"Where it is," Tony said. "Eighth Street. Over east a ways. I've never been there."

"Well," Shapiro said, "you're going to be, Tony. As soon as you can make it. I'll be along. And damn near everybody else, probably. The commissioner, possibly. No, it'll be too early for the commissioner."

"A big one?"

"If they've got it right," Shapiro said. "This evangelist. Or revivalist or whatever they call him. Jonathan Prentis. Been saving cities all over the world. Just finished saving New York."

Tony Cook said he'd be damned and swung his legs out of bed. He still held onto the telephone. "From the outside, this Brawl place looks like what it sounds like. He—hell, it looks like the sort of place he preached against. Last night. Dens of iniquity. Or maybe it was sinks of."

"Don't tell me you've—" Shapiro said, and left it hanging. "Anyway," he said, "it's where he died. If they've got the identity right, and I guess they have. With an ice pick in his back."

"An ice pick, for God's sake!"

"Yes," Shapiro said. "We don't get ice picks much any more. But that's what the precinct says. Ice pick. Anyway, I'll be along. If the subways aren't flooded."

Tony repeated the last word.

"It's raining cats and dogs," Shapiro said. "Here in Brooklyn, anyway."

Tony took the receiver from his ear and listened to other sounds. They were loud sounds, now that he was awake enough to hear them.

"Yeah," he said. "It's sure as hell raining."

He closed the window most of the rain was getting into. Cold wet air came in through it too, before he closed it. He put coffee on and clothes on; strapped his gun on. The big one, this time. The little one was for off-duty hours. He drank coffee and ate toast and put a raincoat on and went out into cold teeming rain. It had been all right when he walked home from Gay Street a little before midnight. Last night it had been almost spring. The wind and rain were coming from the east. The rain blurred the street lights. He walked against the beating rain. It was one hell of a morning. It was the hell of an hour of a hell of a morning. And what, for Christ's sake, had the Reverend Jonathan Prentis been doing in a dive like the Village Brawl? Aside, of course, from getting himself killed in it?

Police cars jammed East Eighth Street. There were four cruise cars and a long sedan. Assistant Chief Inspector Patrick O'Brien, at a guess. Early hours for an assistant chief inspector. But if they were right about who had got himself killed, it was a big one.

Cook said, "Homicide," to a uniformed man in a black slicker who stood at the top of a short flight of steps leading down under a sign which read: "The Village Brawl. Cocktails.

Dancing." The patrolman gestured, and Cook went down the steps. At the foot of the steps there was a glass door with small pictures of naked girls stuck to the glass. A hell of a place for a reverend to die in. Inside the door there was a uniformed police captain. He said, "Oh. The brain boys." Anthony Cook said, "Sir."

The room was large. There was a bandstand at one end with a piano and music racks. Small combo, Tony thought. Piano, a guitar, maybe a trumpet. And the drums, of course. A girl singer? Probably a girl singer; probably an innuendo a lyric.

There was a small dance floor in front of the bandstand. There were tables through the big room and booths along two of the walls. Chairs were upside down on the tables. One of the booths was getting the treatment. Flash bulbs were going off in it. Two men with fingerprint equipment were waiting until the photographers had finished. At a table near the booth, a man from the precinct was talking to a man in a dinner jacket but no black tie.

Tony went over toward the booth and looked into it. No body. He hadn't supposed there would be. The body would be up at Bellevue, in the morgue. Or on a table being opened.

Tony knew the detective talking to the tieless man in the dinner jacket. He started toward the table, and a gray-haired man in a dark suit—and an adhesive bandage on his right jaw—looked at him. Tony said, "Detective Cook, Inspector. Homicide South, sir."

Assistant Chief Inspector Patrick O'Brien said, "Uh," in the tone of a man who is up earlier than he wants to be and has cut himself shaving. Then he added, "About time," and went off toward the uniformed captain at the foot of the entrance stairs.

Tony Cook went to the table where the man from the precinct squad was talking to the man in the dinner jacket. He said, "Morning, Charley." Detective Charles Pieronelli said, "Hi." He said, "All by yourself?"

"Lieutenant Shapiro'll be along," Tony Cook said. "And Captain Weigand, probably."

Tony took a chair off one of the tables and put it down next to Pieronelli. Pieronelli said, "Detective Cook, Mr. Granzo." He said, "Mr. Granzo owns the place, Tony. He's just giving us a rundown, far's he can."

Granzo was a small, neat man. His dinner jacket fitted with precision even when, as now, he leaned forward. He had a light voice when he spoke—a somewhat high-pitched voice.

"Not much I can tell you," Granzo said. "I'd called it a night. Gone upstairs."

He jerked a thumb to show where upstairs was.

"Mr. Granzo has an apartment on the top floor," Pieronelli said, doing his own filling in. "Go ahead, Mr. Granzo."

"This boy came up," Granzo said. "I'd just started to go to bed. It was—oh, maybe two-thirty. Maybe close to three. He banged on the door and I said something. Probably said, 'What the hell?' And he started to jabber through the door. He's Puerto Rican, you see. Knows some English but he was jabbering in Spanish. Very fast. Very excited. Name's Manuel something. He's a bus."

"Manuel Perez," Pieronelli said. "Lives to-hell-and-gone downtown. They're bringing him along. He'd been cleaning up, I take it, Mr. Granzo?"

"With a couple of other boys, yeah. Combo knocks off at two and people begin to drink up and move along. Takes them a while, usually. But about two-thirty the boys begin to stack the chairs on the tables. Sort of a hint. And the waiters who get stuck begin to stand around and look at people. You know how it is."

"Sure," Pieronelli said. "The band's gone and the bar's closed and you—I gather you call it a night, Mr. Granzo. Was it a busy night?"

"Average," Granzo said. "Which is pretty busy. Lot of uptowners come down most nights. Think there'll be hippies, I guess. People from out of town, too. Yeah, we keep pretty busy." He paused. "For now," he said. "Pretty soon they'll start going somewhere else. Way it is in this business."

"This bus boy," Cook said. "Manuel Perez. He knocked at your door. Began, as you say, to jabber at you. You don't understand Spanish, Mr. Granzo?"

"A few words," Granzo said. "A few words of French. For

the waiters. Most of them are Italian. Call themselves Henri and André and things like that, but they're Italian. About Spanish. The kid was all excited. Talking very fast, and I didn't make it out. I let him in and said, 'Speak English, boy,' and he said, 'Dead man. In booth.' Naturally, I thought he was nuts. Thought somebody had had more than he could handle and was sleeping it off."

"But you did go down. Come down here?"

"Yeah. It's my place, after all. Took it over a couple of years ago, when it was a run-down joint. Changed it around some. Man who used to run it had girl waitresses. Believe it or not."

"You serve food here?" Cook asked him.

"Sure. That's the law, isn't it? Suppers, anyway. Mostly people come to drink and dance and listen to Adele. But they can eat if they want to."

"Adele?"

"Girl who sings with the combo. Damn good, too."

"You came down," Pieronelli said, and was patient about it. "This boy showed you the booth he meant. That booth."

He gestured toward the booth halfway down the long wall. The photographers had finished with it. The two fingerprint men were working in it.

"Yeah. This guy was sort of slumped down. Part on the table, part on the seat. You know what I mean?"

They knew what he meant.

"I took hold of his shoulder," Granzo said. "Shook him a little. Said something like—oh, 'We're closing up, sir. Better be getting along.' Something like that."

"And?"

"He sort of slid down on the seat. And then I saw this wooden thing sticking out of his back. Didn't get it, at first. Then I thought, That looks like the handle of an ice pick, for Christ's sake. And then I put my hand on his forehead and he —well, it didn't feel right. Not cold but not warm either. Not the way it ought to have been warm. See what I mean?"

"Yes," Pieronelli said. "We see what you mean, Mr. Granzo. And then you called the police."

"I sure as hell did."

"The call came through at two-fifty-six," Pieronelli told Tony

Cook. "Got a patrol car here in maybe ten minutes. Ambulance maybe another ten minutes. D.O.A. You had seen this man before, Mr. Granzo? Regular customer? Anything like that?"

"Must have seen him when he came in," Granzo said. "People come in, I seat them. When there's a table. But I don't remember this guy. He wasn't a regular. But most of our people aren't. Somebody tells somebody the Brawl is a live spot and they come down to see."

"Reservations?" Tony asked him.

"Mostly no," Granzo said. "They just wander in. From nine o'clock on, mostly. Some come earlier. People who look like out-of-towners. Come for dinner. But mostly it's an after-dinner crowd, like I said."

"Cover charge?"

"Well," Granzo said, "we don't call it that. Say there's a minimum, see? I mean, it's no good having somebody come in for a beer, is there?"

"I can see there wouldn't be," Cook said. "Somebody with him when he came in?"

"Like I said," Granzo said. "I don't remember him at all. Sure, I must have seated him. But I don't remember him. Mostly, people come in couples."

"You'd remember a man who came alone?"

"You'd think so, sure. But thing is, I don't. He was a preacher, right?"

"An evangelist," Pieronelli said. "Revivalist. He's been going pretty much all over the world. Holding gospel meetings. Saving souls. That's what he called it. Saving souls from perdition was the way he put it. Heard him on TV once. Wife held out for it. Week or so ago, that was."

"He had his last meeting at Madison Square Garden last night," Tony said. "Had been going to go on to Chicago and save *it*. Saw him myself, actually."

Charles Pieronelli turned to look at Cook. He said, "Well, I'll be damned, Tony."

"A girl I know held out for it," Anthony Cook said. He looked over Granzo's head. "Austere type, he looked like being," Cook said. "Collar backside front. That sort of thing. Down on drinking. Smoke from cigarettes is smoke from hell fire. Strange place for him to end up." He waved a hand to show what place he meant.

"Listen," Granzo said. "This is an all-right joint. Name of it throws you off, maybe. Called the Village Brawl when I took it over and I let it ride. Damn near all I got for my money, the name of the place. Oh, the lease and some chairs and tables and—"

"Sure," Tony Cook said. "Not throwing off on your place, Mr. Granzo. All I meant was—"

"No pushers," Granzo said. "Keep an eye out for them. No queers, when we can spot them. Few started to show up couple months ago and we had a lot of reserved tables. See what I mean?"

Pieronelli said, "Yes, Mr. Granzo."

"Nice clean boys," Granzo said, with the vigor of a man who wants everything made clear. "Thing is, out-of-towners don't like them. And once they start—well, they sort of take over. Know what I mean?"

This time it was Cook who said, "Yes, Mr. Granzo." Then he said, "This girl singer you have. This Adele. She's—say she's fully dressed?"

"She's decent," Granzo said. "A sweet, decent kid. And she can belt it out. I don't say she's all swaddled up like."

"Chorus line?" Pieronelli said and Granzo turned in his chair and waved a hand toward the small bandstand, raised a few feet from the floor. He said, "There?" He said, "Hell, no. Anyway, that's for uptown. Much as it's for any place nowadays. This is—hell, it's more like being a family place. See what I mean?"

"Sure," Tony Cook said. "Not criticizing your place, Mr. Granzo. Just saying it was an odd place for the Reverend Prentis to come to. Being against liquor and everything. Have his uniform on?"

Granzo shook his head. He said he didn't get it. "Uniform?"

"Clericals," Cook said. "Clerical collar. That sort of thing."

"Hell, no," Granzo said. "Sports jacket, way I remember it.

Sort of greenish, when we put the lights up—like now. Except where—well, where this ice pick or whatever was stuck into him. Only, not very much. Not the way you'd expect."

"Straight into the heart, the ambulance man said," Pieronelli said. "Bled internally. Somebody who knew how to keep from hitting a rib. Only there's plenty of space between ribs. We want any more from Mr. Granzo, Tony?"

"The lieutenant ought to be along pretty soon," Tony Cook said. "Maybe he will. Me, I think we've got the layout for now. Men who come here, Mr. Granzo. They very often wear sports jackets?"

"Some of them do," Granzo said. "Some show up in dinner jackets. They've got to wear neckties, though. This joint's not a joint, see? Not what people call a—"

There was movement at the front of the long room. A uniformed patrolman came down. He had one hand on the shoulder of a small, dark youth with rather long black hair. "That's the Manuel-something kid," Granzo said. "Damn it to hell, he was supposed to get his hair cut yesterday."

The patrolman brought the boy, who had very large dark eyes with, Cook thought, fear in them, over to the table. "Kid who found it," the patrolman said. "Inspector says you may as well get on with it until somebody else shows up. O.K.?"

"O.K.," Pieronelli said.

"Sergeant says they've picked up the waiter," the patrolman said. "Lives to-hell-and-gone up in the Bronx somewhere. Sergeant says, d'you want to talk to him at the station house or shall they bring him over here?"

"Here, I guess," Pieronelli said. He looked at Cook and shrugged his shoulders. Tony Cook had no trouble in interpreting the shrug. There was going to be a lot of fuss made about this one. More of a fuss than a couple of detectives, first grade or not, ought to be stuck with. He began to wonder whether, conceivably, the subways were flooded. Where the hell was—

The glass door with the pictures of naked girls on it opened, and Nathan Shapiro, detective lieutenant, came into the room. Shapiro was tall and thin; his long dark face looked even sadder than usual. Inside he dripped from raincoat to floor. The assistant chief inspector, who had his own raincoat on and was,

Cook thought, probably going home to breakfast, said something to Shapiro and then opened the door and went up the steps. Shapiro came across the room and said, "Morning, Tony," and looked at the others.

"Detective Charles Pieronelli, Lieutenant," Tony said and stood up from his chair. "Precinct squad. Mr. Granzo, who owns the place. And this is the bus boy who found Mr. Prentis."

Shapiro said, "Morning," in a muted voice and took two chairs off a table. He put his wet raincoat on one of them and sat on the other. He said, "Get yourself a chair, son," to the boy with fear in his dark eyes. The boy, who wore a black leather jacket, merely looked at him.

"You speak English, son?" Shapiro asked him.

"Si, sir. Not very good, sir."

"Get a chair and sit down," Shapiro said, his voice low and sad.

The boy got a chair and sat on it. He sat on the edge of it.

"Nothing bad," Manuel Perez said. "I do nothing bad, sir."

"We don't think you did," Shapiro said. "We just want to hear about it."

Manuel turned in his chair and faced Granzo. "Nothing bad," he said. "I didn't do bad thing, Mr. Granzo."

"O.K.," Granzo said. "I'm not going to fire you, kid. Only how often do I have to tell you to get a haircut?"

The boy said something in Spanish, speaking very rapidly. Granzo said, "All right, kid. See that you do." Then he said, "Can't have them going around grubby," to nobody in particular. "Makes the joint look like a joint."

"The boy doesn't look grubby," Shapiro said. "He looks like a nice clean boy. Your name's Manuel, son?"

"Manuel Perez, sir."

"How old are you, Manuel?"

The boy looked quickly at Granzo and then back at Nathan Shapiro. He said, "I'm twenty-one, sir."

He didn't look it, Shapiro thought. He looked, perhaps, seventeen. But it was nothing to make a point of.

"All right," Shapiro said, "tell us about it, son. You were clearing up. By yourself, Manuel?"

"Two others," Manuel said. He held up two fingers. He said, "Sir."

"About what time?"

"All gone," Manuel said. "Everybody gone."

Shapiro looked at Granzo.

"He banged on my door a little before three," Granzo said. "Like I told these gentlemen, I'd just gone up. He—"

"All right," Shapiro said. "Go ahead, son. You were cleaning up. Used glasses. Ashtrays. That sort of thing? Tablecloths?"

"We use mats," Granzo said. "Linen napkins, sure. But mats. Made special for us."

"Mats," Shapiro said. "You were clearing up the booths, Manuel?"

"Si, sir."

"With a tray, or something like that? To put things on?"

"Si, sir. A cart."

"You came to this booth," Shapiro said. He pointed across the room to the booth in which the fingerprint men were still working, using lights. "Then what, son?"

"Man, sir. I said, 'We're closing up, sir.' He didn't say anything and I said, 'Please, sir. We're closed up, sir.' "

"He was sitting at the table. On the bench?"

Manuel answered in Spanish, speaking very rapidly.

"Take it easy, son," Shapiro said. "And in English. I don't understand Spanish. Fine language, but I don't understand it. He was sitting on the bench at the table. And?"

It came more slowly in English. It came with many halts for words.

The man had been sitting on the bench—the bench on the right side as you looked into the booth. He had had his head down on the table. Manuel had thought he was drunk. "On trip, maybe." He had said, "Please, sir," several times. There had been a highball glass, empty, beside the man. He had picked the glass up and put it, with the others, on the cart. There had been only one glass. The man's head had been on the place mat and Manuel, when the man did not answer him, and did not move, had tried to pull the mat out from under the head. The man had moved a little, then, and then Manuel had seen "this thing." The thing was stuck in the man's back. "A thing like Joe uses for the ice, I thought maybe."

Shapiro looked at Granzo.

"The bartender, he means," Granzo said. "We've got an ice machine at the bar, sure, but sometimes the cubes stick together. You know what I mean, Lieutenant?"

"Yes," Shapiro said. "Then, Manuel?"

"I thought something wrong with him. So I ran upstairs to tell Mr. Granzo, sir."

"Right thing to do, son," Shapiro told him. "Earlier on. During the evening. You'd been to this booth? Cleaning ashtrays? Taking off used glasses? That sort of thing?"

"All over," Manuel said. "Lots of people, sir."

"This man," Shapiro said. "You remember whether he was alone in the booth, son?"

"Always two people in the booths, sir. Maybe four people." He held up four fingers.

"So you'd have noticed if this man had been alone in the booth all evening?"

"Maybe, sir. But I all the time running. I work hard, sir. Work good."

"Sure you do," Shapiro said. "So you can't be sure the man was alone?"

"Lots of people," Manuel said. "Lots of tables, sir. And the waiters all the time saying, 'Do this, boy,' 'Do that, boy.' "

"After you had gone upstairs and got Mr. Granzo," Shapiro said. "You came back down with him. Then?"

Sadly, Nathan Shapiro anticipated the answer.

Manuel Perez had finished clearing tables. He had put things on his cart and wheeled the cart into the kitchen, and had taken glasses and plates and knives and forks off it and put them in the dishwasher. And when he and the two other bus boys had filled the dishwasher, one of them had pressed the button and the washer had begun to churn. And the detergent in it to scrub off fingerprints.

Probably, Shapiro thought, it didn't matter. There had been identifying papers in Jonathan Prentis's pockets—an Arkansas driver's license, a social security card, credit cards. Quite enough to go on with.

"Manuel," Shapiro said. "You said a highball glass on the table. Just one?"

"I think so, sir. I think just one."

"All right, son," Shapiro said. "You worked all night. You go home and get some sleep." He turned toward Detective Charles Pieronelli. He said, "We know where he lives, don't we?"

Pieronelli said, "Sure, Lieutenant."

Manuel Perez said, "You mean I go home, sir?"

"Yes," Shapiro said. "That's what I mean, son."

3

It was taking a long time to get the waiter down from the Bronx. But it takes a time to get anybody down from the Bronx to lower Manhattan.

They watched Manuel Perez walk toward the door. He walked, Nathan Shapiro thought, like a boy who expects to be stopped. Shapiro thought of having a police car take the boy home, but he decided against it. A police car would scare the kid. He wouldn't believe the police car was taking him home. Manuel went through the door and up the steps to the sidewalk. He was only a shadow going up the steps but a shadow which moved more quickly.

"The waiters have regular stations?" Shapiro asked Granzo, and Granzo said they did, but that they were shifted—rotated—on stations every week. The man last night?

"Brideaux," Granzo said, "says his first name's André. Tables twenty-two to twenty-eight."

The booth was number?

"That's twenty-two," Granzo said. "B twenty-two. The B's for 'booth.' "

"When the waiter makes out the check," Shapiro said, "I suppose he puts the table number on it? And the number of people served?"

He did. Sure he did. And the checker, who had a table and an adding machine at the end of the bar, checked totals and took money.

"Case anybody pays money," Granzo said. "Mostly it's credit cards. A few charge customers but not many. Damn credit cards. You know they nick us, Lieutenant?"

"Yes," Shapiro said. "Bar checks and food checks are—"

"Only thing," Granzo said, "they bring people in. Damn near got to honor them. What?"

"Bar checks and food checks," Shapiro said. "Two cards? Or all on one? One slip, or whatever you call it?"

"Separate checks," Granzo said. "Stapled together. Joe makes out the drink bills and the waiter the food bills, and Mr. Esposito totals them and writes the total on the back and staples them together."

"Esposito?"

"The checker, Lieutenant. Name's Michael but he likes the 'mister' bit. Married to my sister, Micky is."

"When you close up," Shapiro said. "What does Mr. Esposito do with the paid checks? And the cash? And the charge-card duplicates, of course?"

"Puts them in the safe," Granzo said. "Around noon the bookkeeper comes in and adds things up. See what I mean?"

Shapiro nodded his head.

"I guess we'd better get them out," Shapiro said. "See what Table twenty-two had in the way of drinks. And how many were at the table."

"Listen," Granzo said. "We had maybe a hundred or a hundred and fifty customers last night. And Micky doesn't have time to put them in order. And—"

"Detective Pieronelli'll give you a hand," Shapiro said.

"Also," Granzo said, "we get a turnover. What I mean is, people get finished and somebody else gets the table. See what I mean?"

"Yes," Shapiro said. "Several people may have been at Table twenty-two last night. Detective Pieronelli will help you sort the checks out, Mr. Granzo. You might go along with them, Tony."

Granzo sighed obviously. But he got up and went across the big room and between tables with chairs piled on them and through a wide doorway into, presumably, the service bar. Pieronelli went after him. Pieronelli wasn't as neatly dressed as the man he followed. On the other hand, he was a good deal taller. Cook was last. He was taller than either of the others.

Nathan Shapiro drummed his fingertips on the table and his long sad face grew sadder. This wasn't a case he'd be any good at. That should have been obvious to anybody. This dead man had been a preacher; he had been a Christian preacher. It was the sort of thing which might have ramifications into religion. It would bring Nathan Shapiro up against values, conventions, of which he knew nothing. There would be nuances which he could not be expected to understand. It should go to somebody else, obviously. Bill Weigand himself, for example. Bill was a Christian. He was not, so far as Shapiro knew, very avid about it, but Nathan Shapiro was not especially avid about his own faith. High Holy Days. That about did it. But he was after all the son of a rabbi and that should have been taken into account; should have been taken into account by Captain William Weigand, commanding, Homicide South.

He was always getting assigned to cases beyond his competence. Cases involving painters and theater people, about which he knew no more than he knew of the mores of Christian evangelists. If "evangelists" was what they ought to be called. Bill Weigand was a good cop but one subject to illusions. One of his illusions was Nathan Shapiro, detective lieutenant because of some inexplicable misjudgment on the part of the New York Police Department. Somebody—who was on last night? Oh, sure, Lieutenant Timothy O'Callaghan—had called Weigand at home and waked him up and said that a famous evangelist had been killed in a dive in Greenwich Village and Bill had said, "Get Nate on it."

So. Instead of telling O'Callaghan to get on it himself. O'Callaghan was after all a Christian. Oh, a Roman Catholic, and Catholics, so far as Shapiro knew, did not go in for evangelical drives. (Probably "drive" was the wrong word. "Crusade"?) But there had been Bishop Sheen on television. In robes, as Nate Shapiro dimly remembered from having once, inadvertently, turned him on. Anyway—

Anyway, I've got it for now, Shapiro thought. When we're through here, Bill will be in his office and I'll tell him I'm the wrong man for the job. He sighed, and his long face fell into sadder lines. It wouldn't do any good to explain to Bill Weigand how unsuitable Nate Shapiro was for this particular case. It never had done any good. Because now and then I've been lucky, Nate Shapiro thought, Bill keeps on picking me for jobs I don't belong on.

Shapiro got up from the table and walked over to the booth the fingerprint men had finished with.

The booth was shallow. There were half walls on either side separating it from, presumably, Booths 21 and 23. A narrow table ran through the booth. There were benches on either side. Each bench, he thought, would seat two people if they kept their elbows in close while they ate.

The narrow table was bare, except for traces of the fingerprint dust the technical men had used. Back against the wall there was a small lamp, not lighted. Shapiro reached in and pressed the lamp's button and a dim light came on. Twenty-five-watt, at a guess. Not enough to eat by.

He backed out of the booth and looked up. Yes. Indirect lighting, hidden by wooden baffles. Not too much of it on this gray morning. Less, of course, in the night's darkness.

He leaned down into the booth and peered in the semidarkness at both benches. A precinct detective who had been watching him came over, and he had a flashlight and pointed its beam down on the seat to the right as one entered the booth. There was a little dried blood on the seat. It was at the nearest end of the bench.

"Where he was sitting," the detective said. "Didn't bleed much."

"Enough," Shapiro said. "Internally, I suppose."

The man from the precinct squad said, "Way it looks, Lieutenant."

"This ice pick," Shapiro said. "You see it?"

The detective hadn't. The body had been gone when he got there. But, hell, the lieutenant knew the routine.

Shapiro nodded his head. The routine was set. D.O.A., by the ambulance attendant. Photographs, from all angles. Sketch artist with measurements. Ice pick pulled out, with care about fingerprints, by one of the lab boys and taken to the lab. Body taken to the Bellevue morgue.

Copies of the photographs would, in due course, turn up at Homicide South. They would show a dead man, face down against a table with the wooden handle—or plastic handle—sticking out of his back.

Shapiro stood and looked into the booth, and made up in his mind what the photograph would show.

The Reverend Jonathan Prentis—what size would he be?—leaning forward on the table with the haft of an ice pick sticking out of his back. On the right-hand bench, where the dried blood was. Near the end of the bench closest to the passageway between it and the tables in the middle of the room.

Somebody had leaned into the booth. Prentis had already been leaning forward on the table. Or leaning toward someone sitting opposite him? Or a murderer with an ice pick ready had pushed him forward? Prentis drunk? Or partly drunk? That would show up in the autopsy. Easy to push down on the table? Or resisting of the pressure? The ice pick in his back. Avoiding a rib by luck or knowledge? The murderer's own body shielding the action from people at the tables, from passing bus boys and waiters? And where the hell was the waiter? The Bronx wasn't all that far for a cruise car.

Shapiro went back to the table he had been sitting at and sat at it again. Detectives do a lot of waiting, a lot of it to no purpose.

Cook came back through the wide doorway from the service bar. He put checks down in front of Shapiro.

There were three sets of them, each set a food check and a bar check stapled together.

"Granzo says this order—way the checks are numbered," Cook said. "He's gone upstairs to change. Charley went along to keep him company. Probable order, because the top one they had dinner."

The name of the restaurant was printed at the top of the uppermost check. "The Village Brawl" looked strange in Old English lettering. Below the heading were blanks—"Table No. —," "No. of Persons—," "Waiter No. —."

Table No. 22; No. of Persons 2; Waiter No.? The waiter appeared to be numbered "A" with a wriggly line after it. André? Presumably. And where the hell was André Brideaux? Of course, it was a rain-drenched morning, with visibility low and streets slippery. And a man who has got to bed around three in the morning may be slow in waking up four hours or so later.

The orders were scrawled on the slip. "Two st. well." The word "well" was underlined three times. The two steaks had come to eighteen dollars, plus tax. A hell of a lot of money for two steaks, Shapiro thought.

The bar check stapled to it had, in the same scrawl, "1 dai sw" and "bourb. O.F. g.a." The "dai"—daiquiri?—had cost a dollar and a half. The "bourb. O.F."—bourbon? Old Fitzgerald?—had cost two dollars. The total, written on the back of the bar check, was $21.50 plus $1.28 tax. Quite a lot, Shapiro thought, for a dinner for two, with one drink each. Conceivably, of course, other things had gone with the steak as part of complete dinner. Still—

Shapiro and Cook looked up as a uniformed man came to their table, with a small, dark man walking in front of him. The small man wore a long raincoat, which made him look even smaller. He had a narrow face and a sharp nose and very bright dark brown eyes. The patrolman said, "Mr. Brideaux, Lieutenant. The waiter you wanted to see." Shapiro said, "Thanks," and "Sit down, Mr. Brideaux."

Brideaux said, "M'sieu," and looked at Cook and said it again. Then he sat down. Shapiro said, "Better take that coat off. Looks wet." Brideaux said, "M'sieu," again and stood up and took the coat off and put it on a chair. Under the coat he had worn a pull-over sweater and gray slacks. He sat down again.

"You served Booth twenty-two last night?" Shapiro said.

"And six others," André Brideaux said. "And a couple of outside tables off and on, because Emile got rushed."

He spoke without accent. The "m'sieu" was, Nathan Shapiro decided, a formality; a word to go with "André."

"That where this guy got bumped off?" André said. "Booth twenty-two?"

"Yes," Shapiro said. "Remember how many people you served in that booth last night?"

"Look," André Brideaux said, "we were busy last night. And I had these seven booths to serve and helped Emile on a couple of outside tables. And you've got the checks right there, haven't you, Captain?"

The man was observant, which was a good thing in a witness.

"Yes," Shapiro said, and flipped the check slips over. "A couple," he said. "Another couple. And the third for that table is marked one person. Way you remember it?"

André held out a rather small, very clean hand, and Shapiro gave him the slips, in the order in which they had been given him. André looked at the top slip. He said, "Hell, I sure remember this one, Captain. Man must have weighed in at about two hundred and the woman wasn't much under that. Came in at seven, for God's sake. Minute we opened. Mr. Granzo wasn't down yet. Wasn't hardly anybody around. I had the early trick last night. This isn't much of a dinner place. Mostly people come in, oh, from nine, nine-thirty on. Band starts at nine. But these two out-of-towners—"

They had come in at a few minutes after seven. The hatcheck girl wasn't even on yet. The big man had said, "Don't look very busy, do you?" and André had said, "Most people come a little later, m'sieu. But the kitchen is open." The man had looked around and said, "Where's the band?" André told him it came on later. And the woman had said, "Look, Ralph, we're here, aren't we? Came all the way down here because Mabel and Henry told us about it? And I'm hungry anyway."

André had taken them to Booth 22, because it was on his station.

"Sweet daiquiri," André told Shapiro and Tony Cook. "'And a bourbon with ginger ale. Ginger ale, for God's sake. Old Fitzgerald and ginger ale."

The evident indignation was lost on Shapiro, who drinks sweet wine, and that rarely. It was not wasted on Cook, who said, "Jesus Christ!"

"Yeah," André said. "Makes you wonder don't it?"

They had looked over the menu and the man had said, "These steaks? Porterhouse?"

"I said, boneless sirloin, sir," André told them. "The man said he'd never heard of that and I told him they were fine prime steaks and the woman said, 'Well, we're here, Ralph.' So he said, 'Oh, all right,' or something like that and ordered these drinks of theirs. I had to make the drinks myself because Joe wasn't on yet. And I put in the order for the steaks and got their soup orders and told them what the choice of vegetables was. Last night it was string beans and sprouts, and they both took the sprouts."

He had an excellent memory, Shapiro thought. He didn't give a damn what this couple had had to eat, but it is a good thing to encourage an excellent memory.

André had brought the steaks and, "This guy cut into his and it was a little pink and he said, 'Hey, you, I said we wanted them well done. You didn't hear me, maybe?' "

André had taken the steaks back to the kitchen and the chef had made violent sounds—"They get upset easy, these chef types"—and cooked the steaks until they were gray all through. The man had said, "More like it," and "Where's the ketchup? Ought to be on the table."

André had got the ketchup.

"I'd got them French fries," André said. "He put ketchup on them."

There was something like a shudder in his voice. He looked at Cook and shook his head. Cook obliged him. Cook said, "Jesus!"

"Yeah," André said. "On the French fries, *And* the steak."

He looked at Cook again and Cook said, "Takes all kinds, they say," but without any conviction.

The couple had finished their dinner—both had had ice cream with chocolate sauce for dessert—at a little after eight. By that time other waiters had come on and there were a few other customers. Drinking customers. André had brought the big couple their checks and the big man had checked the addition very carefully and said, "Where's the cashier's desk? Didn't see it when we came in."

"On the check," André told Cook and Shapiro, "it says, 'Please pay waiter.' I showed him what it said and he said something like it was a funny way to do things, and gave me a fifty-dollar bill. Took all the small bills Mr. Esposito had, pretty near, it being so early in the evening. He counted it all twice and I thought he was going to leave me just the silver, but the woman said, 'That's not enough, Ralph. You know how they are in New York.' Something like that. So he left me a dollar."

It was obvious that the memory shook him. Shapiro gave him a few seconds to recover and then said, "After that? In Booth twenty-two, I mean?"

André went to the second check and his face brightened.

"Nice couple of kids," he said. "Maybe about nine-thirty. Celebrating something, way it looked. Champagne. *Brut.* And after they'd danced a while, chicken sandwiches and another half bottle. Nice kids. Thought they were going to make a night of it, but a little after eleven they left."

"Do better this time?" Cook asked him, and André slid the slip across the table to him.

"Paid American Express," André said. "Wrote the tip in."

The tip had been written in. It was a sizable check. The tip was somewhat over 20 per cent of it.

"They were sure nice kids," André said. "I'd figured they were celebrating something and were going to make a night of it."

"Perhaps they did," Shapiro said "Now, Mr. Brideaux. This last customer."

"André, Captain. Just André."

"All right, André," Shapiro said. "This last man in Booth twenty-two?"

André went to the last check for Booth 22.

"I see," Shapiro said, "You put a 'one' in the number-of-persons place. So I take it he was alone?"

André looked for some seconds at the slip. He looked up at Nathan Shapiro and down at the slip again. But there was nothing evasive in his look across at Shapiro. There was merely, Shapiro thought, momentary uncertainty. André looked at the face of the check and then nodded his head.

"Tall man?" André said. "Tall and black hair and—oh, sort of rigid? That the man, Captain? The man somebody killed?"

"I don't know what he looked like," Shapiro said. "I haven't seen the photographs yet and—"

"Yeah," Tony Cook said, "That's what he looked like, Nate. From a distance, anyway."

Shapiro looked at him.

"I went to this meeting of his last night," Cook said. "What they call a gospel meeting."

There was a defensive note in his voice, Nathan Shapiro thought. Shapiro merely nodded his head.

"Miss Farmer wanted to go," Cook said. "It was quite a show."

Shapiro nodded his head again.

"He had a voice like nothing I'd ever heard," Cook said. "Deep and—I don't know. Rich, I guess. Like—hell, I don't know. Seemed to be all over the Garden, if you know what I mean. Gave you a sort of funny feeling. As if you were hearing something you'd never heard before."

"Were you, Tony?"

Tony Cook shook his head.

"That New York is a sink of iniquity," Tony said. "That everybody in it is going to hell unless they accept the Lord. At first it sounded—I don't know. Sounded different because of this voice of his. After a while I didn't listen much and—well, got to thinking it was going to be a hell of a job to get a cab if we waited until everybody left. So we—well, we went home. I mean, back to Miss Farmer's apartment."

He was overexplaining, Shapiro thought and was a little amused. But his smile was inward, where his smiles usually hide themselves.

"Same man," André said. "Anyway, there was something sort of special about his voice. Tall, black hair and this voice. Pretty sure it was the same man. Came in by himself. That's why I put 'one' down for the number of guests."

"Came in alone," Shapiro said. "About when, André?"

André Brideaux shrugged.

"Maybe eleven-thirty," he said. "Some time around then. The jo—the place was hopping. Way it usually is about then."

"Mr. Granzo seat him?"

"No. It's come back now. The boss was seating a foursome. One of the men he knew, way it looked. And this guy came up to the rope and I had a minute and I said, 'One, sir?' And he said, 'Two, please, I'm expecting a friend to join me.' So twenty-two was free and I took him there and gave him the supper menu and asked him if he wanted to order or wait for his friend. He said I could bring him a Scotch on the rocks with a little water on the side. So I did. That's when I put the 'one' on the check."

"He was still alone when you brought the drink back?"

"Yes, m'sieu."

"But later?"

"Later," André said, "it was a hell of a rush, Captain. And Emile got jammed up and I was helping him. Way we do it, one of us gets in a jam anybody who's free helps him out. See what I mean? People get all jumbled up, like."

He looked at the check on the table in front of him.

"Six Scotches," he said. "Must have been somebody with him. Part of the time, anyway. He—wait a minute. Way it was—"

The way it was, as André remembered it, he had been passing Booth 22 and the tall man had raised a glass and then raised two fingers. So André had gone to the bar for two more Scotches and had brought them back to the booth. The man had still been alone in it, but he had gestured across the table and André had put one Scotch in front of him and the other on the mat across from him. "It was set up for two," André said.

"I figured this friend of his had shown up," André said. "And—oh, gone to the men's, or something. Or seen somebody he knew at another table and gone to say hello to him. Place like this, people wander around a good deal."

"You say 'gone to the men's,'" Shapiro said, "This friend of his was a man, then?"

Suddenly, André hit himself on the forehead with the flat of his hand. He said, "Captain, I'm nuts. The friend sure as hell wasn't a man. It was a girl. I went by and looked in to see if they wanted something, and here was this girl across from him. A real dish, she was. I must be going nuts not to have remembered."

"You were busy," Shapiro said. "Can you remember what this girl looked like?"

André slapped his forehead again, not so hard this time. Then he shook his head.

"Blonde, I think," he said. "All I thought was, He's got himself a dish, all right. But they didn't need fresh drinks yet and I had a lot who did. Pretty sure she was a blonde. And built. I know damn well she was stacked."

"You served them another round," Shapiro said. "Two more, since they had six altogether."

"Took their order," André said. "Same again. But I was really jammed up and Emile wasn't, and I said, 'Mind giving these to twenty-two, sir?' And he said—oh, I don't know. That he sure would. Anyway, he did, because when I went by the next time they both had pretty full glasses."

"They seemed to be getting along all right?"

"Far's I could tell. They were talking, I guess. Look, Captain, I was rushed. Job like this, you get the customers what they want. You don't look at them much."

"This young couple," Cook said. "The ones who ordered champagne. Apparently they made more of an impression on you."

"We weren't so busy then," André said. "And they were sweet kids. It was like they were celebrating something. It—well, it sort of shone out of them, know what I mean? And I had a sort of lull then. Not like later."

"The man—the tall man we're talking about—had a drink," Shapiro said. "Then he ordered two more, and the girl wasn't there yet. Or was leaving her coat or something. Then, when they were both in the booth together, he ordered another round and Emile took the drinks over. That comes to five, so far."

"Yeah, he ordered one more later. She—I remember that—put her hand over her glass and shook her head."

"Any idea how much later, André?"

André shrugged his shoulders. Then he said, "Maybe around one. Maybe after one. They didn't drink fast. Except maybe he did the first one."

"He got here some time around eleven-thirty," Shapiro said. "Any idea how much later the girl came? I mean, when he ordered another drink for himself and one for her. When you thought she probably was leaving her coat at the check room?"

"Maybe half an hour, Captain."

"And they were still there after one, when she refused a drink."

"About then, Captain. The combo plays until two, see. And we've got this minimum, so they don't save anything by rushing off."

"What is the minimum, André?"

After nine, when the music started, the minimum was five dollars a person. Most people went over it.

"What do the drinks cost, André? The Scotches?"

"Two and a half a throw. But it's an honest two ounces, Captain."

"So their drinks came to fifteen dollars."

"Plus tax, Captain."

"Well over the minimum. I take it he paid you."

He had beckoned. André thought it probably had been close to two. Anyway, things had begun to slow down. André had gone to the table and given the man a check. He had been alone in the booth. André had assumed the girl had gone to the ladies' to freshen up. The man had given him a twenty-dollar bill. He had tipped two dollars. He had remained sitting in the booth, and André had assumed he was waiting for the girl to come back.

"Last you saw of him?"

It had been, André said. He himself had come on early and so he got off early. At a little after two.

"You didn't see the girl again?"

He had not. He had got off early and gone home by subway.

"The man—his name was Prentis—seemed all right when he paid? Sober enough, I mean? He'd had four drinks, after all."

"He seemed all right. After all, Captain, they'd spaced the drinks out."

"Eleven-thirty or so until almost two," Shapiro said. "Yes. You didn't see anybody stop by the booth at any time?"

"And stick this ice pick into him? Listen, Captain. Wouldn't I have told you?"

Shapiro was sure he would have. He supposed that, when the place was full, people moved around a good deal? Left their tables to go to the dance floor? Perhaps did some table-hopping?

"Sure. They all the time bump into you if you aren't careful."

"Did Mr. Prentis—the Reverend Mr. Prentis—and the girl dance?"

André answered that merely with a shrug.

Shapiro looked at Tony Cook and raised dark eyebrows.

"This man was dressed just like anybody else?" Cook asked André.

"Look," André said, "they dress all sorts of ways. Dinner jackets even."

"Sure," Tony said. "This man, André. Not dressed like a minister. I mean, black suit, turned-around collar."

"Just like a lot of them," André said. "Jacket. Tweed maybe. You don't notice too much when the lights are down. The way they are when we're open."

4

But Jonathan Prentis, however he had dressed at the Village Brawl, had not been just like anybody. Nathan Shapiro thought of that, sadly, as a patrol car took him and Tony Cook uptown and cross-town to West Twentieth Street, and the headquarters of Homicide South. Prentis had been important; he had been what people called a "personality." In the early days of his revival meetings—what he had called his "gospel meetings"—the New York *Times* and the *Daily News* had carried stories about them. (The *Times* on the split page.) They had kept a tally of those "saved." The first of the meetings had been carried live on the local television station, and there had been taped excerpts in news reports.

Shapiro had been vaguely conscious of this. He had not watched the telecasts. He prefers symphonies on FM radio. He had skimmed the news stories. But he knew enough about Prentis to know what was coming now. It would be, for the newspapers and radio and television reporters, a big one. And he would be in the middle of it. Oh, they would start at the top, of course—start with the assistant chief inspector in charge of the detective division. But they would work down to him. And, this time, they would discover his incompetence.

He had been a patrolman walking a beat, or riding in a patrol car, in Brooklyn. He had been a detective (3rd gr.) on a precinct squad in the Bronx. He envied the younger Nathan Shapiro who was not often thrust into situations which emphasized his inadequacy. What it comes down to, he thought, as the car turned up Eighth Avenue, I'm pretty good with a gun. That should all along have been evident to—

"A hell of a funny place for him to get it," Tony Cook said. "A dive, really. Oh, a hell of an expensive dive. But a place that sells spirituous liquors."

"Spirituous liquors?" Shapiro said. It didn't sound like Tony Cook.

"What he called the stuff," Tony said. "Very down on it last night. At the meeting, I mean. First glass of beer is the first step down to hell. Look not upon the wine when it is red. Strong drink is a mocker. Went on for maybe ten minutes. Also, cigarettes. The fumes from hell."

Reminded, Tony Cook lighted himself a cigarette.

"And he gets himself killed in a joint with half a dozen Scotches inside him," Cook added, when the cigarette burned evenly.

"Four," Shapiro said. "The girl had two. From about eleven-thirty until about two, if the waiter's right. And is spilling all he knows, of course."

"You think he isn't?"

"No. Everything he remembers, I think. A lot to fill in, of course."

Which was obvious to them both. Routine would try to fill it in—the detectives of the precinct squad would try to fill it in. There was a waiter named Emile, whose station was near Booth 22. There were half a dozen other waiters. There were the bus boys and the hat-check girl. There were, if they could be tracked down, customers of the Village Brawl. (That would be pretty hopeless, except for a few who might have charge accounts; who might be known to Angelo Granzo.)

Somebody might have seen something. Might have seen a man bending into a booth. It would take a lot of detectives to find out; a lot of doorbell ringing; a lot of trudging.

"This girl who sings there," Tony said. "Adele something."

"Lorraine," Shapiro said. "Adele Lorraine. Yes, up on the platform. Singing to the customers. A vantage point to see things from. A job for the precinct boys. It's a good squad, Tony."

Tony Cook said, "Sure," in the tone of a man who is thinking of something else. "Speaking of girl singers—"

The car stopped in front of the West Twentieth Street station. They got out of it and the patrolman driver saluted, not very seriously. They flicked hands at him.

"Of girl singers?" Shapiro said, as they climbed a stairway.

"Rachel knows a girl who sings in the choir," Tony said. "This revival choir. Did until last night, anyway. Not that that would get us anywhere. Somebody they hired locally. Sings in nightclubs when she can get jobs, Rachel says. Only thing is, she might know people. Probably just other choir singers. Might have heard—oh, bits and pieces floating around. Like the Reverend Prentis not being quite so holy as he made out. As he apparently wasn't."

"Not by his standards," Shapiro said. "You, Tony. You know the name of this choir singer?"

Tony did not. All right, he could find out. Only—he looked at his watch. The time was eight-thirty-nine.

"She won't like it," he said. He was told there was no hurry; that it was a hundred to one the girl wouldn't have anything that would help them.

"Thing is," Tony said, "Rachel has a lot of jobs. Here, there and everywhere. Once she's gone out she's damn hard to catch up with."

He spoke, Shapiro thought, from the experience of a man who has tried. He thought it understandable. Urged, Tony had brought Rachel for dinner to the Shapiro apartment in Brooklyn, and Rose had liked her. "Offbeat," Rose had said. "Her generation is, Nathan. From the viewpoint of ours. But a nice kid, I think."

Rose, assistant principal of a high school in Greenwich Village, was in contact with the generation which reached up toward Rachel Farmer's. She could tell the "nice" ones from those not so nice. At any rate, Nathan Shapiro was certain she could. He has implicit confidence in Rose's judgment. She was wrong about Nathan Shapiro, of course, but right about almost everything else. She thought Nathan was as intelligent as his father had been, which was nonsense—agreeable nonsense, but nonsense all the same. Rabbi Emmanuel Shapiro had been a great man.

Captain William Weigand, commanding, was not yet in his office at Homicide South, so Nathan Shapiro could not, once more, stress his unfitness for the investigation assigned. Shapiro went to his own small office. What had so far come through was scrappy, added little. Jonathan Prentis had been an ordained minister of the Evangelical Disciples Church; he had been fifty-one years old; he was a native of the state of Arkansas. He had attained nationwide fame as an evangelist some ten years ago; he had carried his crusade across the Atlantic five years or so later. London had been responsive, at least in attendance. Edinburgh had not. He had not preached in Paris. On the West Coast of the United States, particularly in the Los Angeles area, the crowds who went to hear him had needed police control. Chicago had been almost equally responsive, and the police had found vigorous action necessary. Nobody had been killed and only thirty or so had needed hospitalization.

He had been preaching in New York for three weeks, and last night's meeting was to have been the last of the series. He had preached three times a week—Wednesdays, Fridays and Sundays for the most part, if the New York Rangers were not playing home games.

His permanent address had been "The Tabernacle, Little Rock, Arkansas." In New York it had been the Hotel Wexley, on Broadway in the Seventies.

He had been married, for a little more than ten years, to Hope Pruitt Prentis. They had no children.

All scrappy; all hurriedly scraped together from newspaper files and, presumably, *Who's Who in America*. Not enough for a picture to form, for any coherence to form. A glossy print of a man slumped forward on a table in a restaurant booth; a close-up of a piece of wood protruding from the left side of his back. Piece of wood about three inches long, at a guess. Attached to a pointed rod about four inches long, probably. But it would, by now, have been measured. It would have been checked for fingerprints. Probably, from the photograph, without substantial result. Rough wood, from the picture. Good prints rarely come from rough wood.

Check in with Weigand, who would be in any minute, and make his pitch. And get nowhere with it and pick up Tony Cook and go up to a hotel on upper Broadway and ask people questions. His telephone rang. He said, "Shapiro," and then, "All right, Bill. I'll be right along."

At his desk in the squad room, Tony Cook looked at his watch again. It still lacked several minutes of being nine in the morning. She wouldn't be pleased. All right. Not Tony calling. Detective (1st gr.) Anthony Cook, of Homicide South.

He dialed a familiar number. He listened to the signal which told him that a telephone bell was shrilling in a second-floor apartment in Gay Street. A telephone within easy reach of a wide bed. He knew. Once or twice he had had to reach for it across a long and slender girl.

The telephone rang four times. She couldn't already be up and away. Or even up and making coffee. Or—

" 'Lo?"

The voice was weighted down, blurred, by sleep.

He said, "Tony. I'm sorry as hell, but—"

"Mister," Rachel Farmer said, "go back to sleep. It isn't even dawn yet."

"Darling," Tony said, "I'm sorry as hell."

"The thing is," she said, and some of the sleep had gone out of her voice, "you only just left. So it can't be—is it raining or something? It sounds as if—"

"Raining," he said. "Reason it's still so dark. Are you all right?"

"Mister," Rachel said, "how can I tell? At this hour?" There was a momentary pause and a slight rustling sound. She was, he thought, sitting up in bed. He could see her sitting up in bed. It was a distracting thing to see.

"All right," Rachel said. "I'm awake now. And, yes, I'm all right. Is that what you called up to ask me?"

"No," he said. "A man's been killed."

"Not by me," Rachel said. "Oh—anybody we know, Tony?"

"The man we heard last night," he said. "The preacher. In a place called the Village Brawl over on Eighth Street."

"Rather a gyp joint," she said. "In an expensive sort of way. I wasn't there last night, dear. You must have a very short memory."

"No," he said. "My memory's fine." He tried to remember that he was Detective (1st gr.) Anthony Cook. And to quit thinking about a girl who never wore anything at night sitting up in bed. He said, "Listen, Rachel," and was unhappy about the sternness which seemed to have come into his voice.

"The Reverend something Prentis has been killed," she said. "I'm listening, mister. At nine o'clock on a rainy morning when I was sound asleep."

"I said I was sorry," he told her. "I am sorry. Last night you said you knew a girl who sang in this revival choir."

"When she couldn't get nightclub spots," Rachel said. "Yes. Jan Rushton."

"Jan?"

"Oh, I suppose for Janet. You don't think she killed him, do you? Because she seems to be a nice kid. I don't know her very well, but she's a nice blonde kid. How did this man get killed?"

"With an ice pick."

"It doesn't sound like her," Rachel Farmer said. "Not at all like her. She's too young to know about ice picks. They went out—oh, when I was a very little girl. Ages ago."

He said, "Not ages, for God's sake," because Rachel's voice—and the mental picture of her sitting up in bed—distracted him. "You're only—"

She laughed at him, but laughed gently. She said, "It's too early in the morning, dear. And you're too far away. About Jan Rushton?"

He said, "A blonde? Good-looking?"

"Cute anyway. Yes, blonde hair. And blue eyes. I've only met her a couple of times at parties."

"Type who would play around?"

"I wouldn't wonder. You like little ones with blue eyes and blonde hair, Tony?"

"You know the kind—" he said, and caught himself and said, "No, Rachel," in an impersonation of a policeman's voice. "Do you know where she lives?"

"In Washington Place, I think. I don't know the number. I'm not even sure it's Washington. It could be Waverly. I told you I've only met her a couple of times. Listen, you were at one of the parties yourself. You must have met her."

"I never remember little girls with blue eyes and blonde hair," he told her, and thought, By God, recently that's been true. "Washington Place. Or perhaps Waverly Place. Do you happen to know whether she shares the apartment, or the room or whatever, with somebody?"

"No, Tony. But she'll have a telephone. And she'll be in the book, because an agent might call any time and have a big offer. Is she supposed to be a witness or something?"

"I doubt it," Tony said. "A source of information, maybe. Will you have dinner with me tonight, lady?"

"Well, we had dinner last night."

"Last night we had hamburgers and went to be saved. Tonight?"

"Yes, mister. And there's a movie at the Eighth Street. Seven, about?"

"If we've got to go to a movie," Tony said, "and are going to have a decent dinner, six-thirty."

She said, "All right, mister. I've got to put some clothes on and go out in the rain to a place full of drafts and take them off again. Six-thirty."

There was only one Rushton, Janet, in the Manhattan book. She did live on Washington Place. But she did not answer her telephone, although he let it ring a dozen times.

He got up from his desk when Detective Lieutenant Nathan Shapiro came into the squad room. Nate looks even sadder than usual, Tony thought. He's made his pitch to the captain —the pitch that he'll be no good at this one. And the captain has brushed him off again. He walked toward Nathan Shapiro and Nathan raised dark eyebrows, sadly, in question.

"Name's Janet Rushton," Cook said. "Lives on Washington Place, down in the Village. In the phone book. Doesn't answer the phone."

"Probably wouldn't have anything to tell us if she did," Shapiro said. "You can try her again later."

Cook followed Shapiro down the stairs from Homicide South. At the bottom of the stairs, he said, "She's a blonde, Rachel says."

"The town's full of them," Shapiro told him, and led the way into a police sedan. They went up the West Side Drive and left it at Seventy-second and went cross-town to Broadway and up it a few blocks.

The Hotel Wexley was ten stories high. It had the sedateness of age. The space in front of it was marked "Loading Area. No Parking." There were two cruise cars and a sedan marked "Police" against the curb and the lab car double-parked outside them. The driver from the West Twentieth Street car pool pulled behind the lab car, and Shapiro and Cook got out into the rain. It was raining harder than ever. A cold wind hurled rain at them. A week ago it was supposed to start being spring, Tony thought.

There was a patrolman, dressed for the weather, outside the main door of the Hotel Wexley. He said, "Morning, sir," to Shapiro. He said, "Sixth floor."

The lobby was large and empty. At the far end of it an electric sign said, "Coffee Shop," and there were a few people in it having breakfast. Outside the coffee shop a man was running a vacuum cleaner back and forth on the carpet.

Tony pushed the "up" button for an elevator—any one of four elevators. Above the elevator doors there were dials with pointers, and according to the pointers all the elevators were going up. But then, although the pointer was fixed at "10," the door of one of the elevators slapped open and a man came out of it, preceded by a Scotty on a leash. The Scotty sniffed Shapiro's trouser legs and then looked up and widened his mouth in what was either a snarl or a grin. He didn't say anything. The man he was leading said, "Come on, you," and they went toward the hotel door.

"Smelled Cleo," Tony said as he pressed the "6" button in the car. Tony had met the Shapiros' Scotty bitch. Shapiro said, "Mmmm," and the car stopped and, after a pause, the door opened. A heavily built man with an unexpectedly narrow and sharp face came out of a room opposite the elevator and said, "Morning, Nate. Couple of your boys here already."

Shapiro said, "Morning, Frank," to Francis X. Maloney, acting captain, commanding the precinct detective squad. "Maxwell and Smith." Maloney said, "How's Bill Weigand?" and Shapiro said, "Fine. Up to his ears." Maloney said, "Who isn't?" and then waved toward the door he had come out of.

"They've got the whole floor," Maloney said. "Seems to be the central office, far's I can tell. We just got here ourselves."

"The wife?" Shapiro said.

Maloney gestured down the corridor. He said, "Been told. One of the girls's with her. They had separate rooms, incidentally. Opposite sides of the hall. Both corner rooms."

"One of the girls" would be a policewoman. Probably a detective third. If that, she would do more than hold the hand of the bereaved and say, "There, there, dear." If Mrs. Jonathan Prentis wasn't hysterical, or otherwise in shock, the detective, third grade, would be getting information out of her.

"In there?" Shapiro said, and pointed toward the open door across from the elevators.

"A priest or something," Maloney said. "I guess they don't call them priests, but he's got a priest's collar, sort of. Chief assistant, he says he was. Name of Higgs." He paused and shook his head. "John Wesley Higgs," he said, and shook his head again. Then, apparently to himself, he added, "Holy Mother of God!" Once more he shook his head. "Talks like he wrote the Holy Scriptures," he said, this time to Nathan Shapiro.

"This girl," Shapiro said. "The one with Mrs. Prentis?"

"Name of Grace Flanders," Maloney said. "Just made detective. Nice, hard-working kid."

"You might go along and sit in, Tony," Shapiro said. "Give Detective Flanders a hand if she needs one."

Cook said, "O.K., Lieutenant," and went off down the corridor. Shapiro said, "The setup?" to Acting Captain Maloney.

"Like I said," Maloney told him, "we just got here. But somebody had waked up early and listened to news on the radio. And passed the word along. So, when I got here, they were popping in and out of doors and some of them were crying and saying, 'No, no!' That sort of thing. Must be—hell, there must be twenty of them on the floor. Maybe more. Haven't had a chance to straighten them out. There's a choir leader and someone they call the director and the fund chief—that's what they call her. Kind of a treasurer or bookkeeper or something. And a lot of other women, mostly middle-aged. Secretaries, typists. I don't know. And this man Higgs. This chief assistant."

"A place to start," Shapiro said, and went across the corridor. He partly closed the open door to the "central office." On the outside of it there was a metal plaque, supported by a chain. It read: "The Reverend Jonathan Prentis. Minister of the Gospel. Come Unto Jesus."

Shapiro went into the room.

It was, apparently, the living room of a suite. There were doors on either side, both closed. It appeared to have been refurnished as an office. The desk was an office desk; the steel filing cabinet at right angles to it was an office filing cabinet. The man sitting behind the desk was a small man in clericals—a small, thin man with a narrow face and eyes set narrowly together. His clerical collar was, Shapiro thought, large for him—large by at least two sizes. Threatened, Shapiro thought, the Reverend Higgs could retract his head into the collar.

Maloney said, "This is Lieutenant Shapiro, Reverend. From the Homicide Squad. This is the Reverend Higgs, Nate. He feels we must have made a mistake."

Shapiro said, "Mistake?" and pulled a chair up and sat facing John Wesley Higgs across the desk. "How a mistake, Mr. Higgs?"

"In identifying the man who has been killed as the Reverend Prentis," Higgs said. He had a harsh, somewhat croaking voice. "He would never have been in a—a nightclub. Where liquor is served. Where lasciviousness is permitted."

Shapiro repeated "lasciviousness?" with a rising inflection.

"Dancing," Higgs said, and on that word his voice seemed harsher. "Have you been saved, Lieutenant?"

"Not in the sense you mean, Mr. Higgs," Shapiro said. "Or that I take it you mean. I am a Jew, Mr. Higgs. My father was a rabbi."

Which has nothing to do with anything, Nathan Shapiro thought. Except my being the wrong man for this job.

"God's mercy encompasseth all of His children," Higgs said, apparently in consolation.

Shapiro said, "Mmmm." He said, "I'm afraid there's no real doubt about the identification, Mr. Higgs. Unless, of course, somebody had stolen Mr. Prentis's wallet and all his papers. We don't think it was that way, Mr. Higgs. A tall man with dark hair, Mr. Prentis? Handsome in an austere sort of way?"

"He is a man of God, Lieutenant," Higgs said. "I suppose he could be described as you describe him. But he would never have gone to a place like that. That is beyond belief. I have known him since we were young men together, working together in the vineyards. He would never enter a place of iniquity."

Acting Captain Maloney had not come into the room with Shapiro. He had closed the door after Shapiro and remained in the corridor. Now he opened the door and leaned in. He said, "Fingerprint boys have finished up, Nate. Plenty to match the ones they brought with them."

"The ones from the corpse?" Shapiro said and was looked at in surprise.

"Sure," Maloney said. "What the hell, Nate?"

"Mr. Higgs seems to feel we've made a mistake in identity," Shapiro said. "That Mr. Prentis would never have been in a place like the Village Brawl."

"Well," Maloney said, "he sure as hell was."

He went back out into the corridor and closed the door.

"So, Mr. Higgs," Shapiro said. "There can't be any doubt, can there? Not with papers and now fingerprints matching. So he was there, Mr. Higgs. And was killed there."

Higgs shook his head. He said again that it was beyond belief. His voice remained harsh, but it was less emphatic.

Shapiro waited.

"Unless," Higgs said, and shook his head again. He did not go on for several seconds and Shapiro said, "Yes, Mr. Higgs?"

"Our mission takes us often into strange places," Higgs said. "For the salvation of souls. Into the homes of the rich and of the poor. Even, sometimes, into places of degradation. Such as this—what was the name of this place?"

"It's called the Village Brawl," Shapiro said.

"It wasn't clear on the radio," Higgs said. "Or, if I heard it, I couldn't believe it."

Shapiro had had a little difficulty in believing it himself when he had answered his telephone in the Brooklyn apartment.

"The name of it," he told Higgs, who kept on shaking his head. "A restaurant and nightclub. Rather large. Quite expensive. Operated legally. At least, we've had no complaints about it. You mean Mr. Prentis might have—" He groped momentarily for words. "Might have gone there with someone whose soul needed saving? Or—gone to preach there?"

"To wrest a soul from the devil," Higgs said. "He was a man of God. We are called sometimes to strange places, Lieutenant. Into sordid places. To wrestle with the devil in places where he reigns. It is the only explanation. Yes, that is believable. Was he alone in this place of evil?"

"Apparently not," Shapiro said. "According to one of the waiters, he had a young woman with him. For part of the time, anyway."

"A woman of the streets," Higgs said. "Whom he was seeking to turn from her evil ways."

"We don't know who she was," Shapiro said. "Or what kind she was. He had a few drinks with her. That we do know."

"No," Higgs said. "That cannot be. It is a sin to drink spirituous liquors. Wine is a mocker, strong drink is raging. That is from Scripture. Proverbs nineteen, verse one."

"Proverbs twenty, I think," Nathan told him. "But no doubt you're right. And the waiter may, of course, have been mistaken."

The blood tests wouldn't be; the blood tests would show alcohol. But there was nothing to be gained by pointing this out to the small, harsh-voiced man of faith.

"Mr. Prentis had a meeting last night," Shapiro said. "At Madison Square Garden. Were you there, Mr. Higgs?"

"Of course. I was always with him. It was a magnificent meeting, Lieutenant. A hundred and ninety-six came forward to accept Christ. Little children. And men and women long steeped in sin. There was rejoicing in heaven."

"Yes," Shapiro said. "The meeting lasted until about when, Mr. Higgs?"

"About ten, I think."

"Then?"

Higgs shook his head.

"What did Mr. Prentis do then?" Shapiro said. "If you know."

"Oh," Higgs said. "We came back here. Back to the hotel. The Reverend Prentis and Mr. Farmington and I."

"By taxi?"

"In the limousine, of course. The one we rent. The strain of the meetings, the *exaltation* of the meetings, drain the Reverend Prentis." He paused for a moment. "Drained," he said. "If it is true that he has passed on."

"I'm afraid it is," Shapiro said. "Came back here, the three of you in the car. Then?"

"I retired," Higgs said. He gestured toward one of the doors. He said, "My bedroom is there. Mr. Farmington has the other room." He motioned toward the other door.

"Mr. Farmington?"

"The choir leader. And the soloist. He was, I think, a singer in the opera before he found salvation. He is a man of dedication."

"Last night," Shapiro said. "Did he go to bed too, Mr. Higgs?"

"I believe he stopped downstairs for a cup of coffee," Higgs said. "He sometimes does."

"And Mr. Prentis himself?"

"He said good night, as he always did. He said, 'May God watch over you.' He went down toward his room."

"He was still in uni—I mean in clerical clothing?"

"Yes. He wore it at all times, of course. As an outward demonstration of his inward dedication."

"He was an ordained minister?"

"Certainly. We graduated from the seminary together. Were ordained at the same time."

"In what congregation?" Nathan Shapiro asked, and thought that that probably was the wrong word. "Denomination, I mean."

"Evangelical Disciples, Lieutenant. We believe Holy Scripture to be the Word of God." He looked at Shapiro rather sharply. "In all respects," he said. "We are what some more frivolous call fundamentalists."

"You'd worked with Mr. Prentis for many years? Since you both were ordained?"

That was not entirely true. They had drifted apart for a time. Higgs had been "called" to a small church in southern

Arkansas. Prentis to a considerably larger one in Tennessee. Prentis had, after a few years as pastor of his church, embarked on his "evangelical mission."

"I sought at one time to follow in his footsteps," Higgs said. "I had not his gifts. I heard him preach in—Memphis, I think it was. I asked whether I could not aid him. He permitted it. That was many years ago."

Shapiro said he saw. He said, "According to Captain Maloney, you were his chief assistant."

"Ours is a large mission," Higgs said. "There are many details. I helped with those. Tried to spare him those."

"Yes," Shapiro said. "How, Mr. Higgs? I'm just trying to get the picture. Arranged transportation? That sort of thing?"

"No," Higgs said. "Those matters are in the hands—the very capable hands, Lieutenant—of Theodore Acton. I helped him with his sermons. With the articles he wrote for newspapers and magazines. In a most modest way. The inspiration was always his, of course."

Higgs was, Shapiro thought, making rather a point of his unimportance, of the smallness of his contribution.

"His was the voice," Higgs said, adding to it. "The inspiring Voice." His inflection supplied a capital to "voice."

And yours the words? Shapiro wondered, and thought it could make no difference.

"To get back to last night," he said. "Mr. Prentis went to his room. He was still in clericals, of course. You went to bed. And to sleep at once?"

"Almost."

"Mr. Farmington? You said he stayed downstairs for coffee. Did you hear him come in?"

"No. He would have moved very quietly. He is a considerate man."

"By the way," Shapiro said. "Where is he now, do you know?"

"One of us was asked to go with the police to identify—identify Mr. Prentis," Higgs said. "They suggested Mrs. Prentis, but she was in no condition to undertake so shattering a task. So it was agreed that the duty—the sad duty—should devolve on Mr. Farmington."

A wordy man, Shapiro thought. But he knew nothing about men like this.

"Speaking of Mrs. Prentis," he said. "I understand she and Mr. Prentis have separate rooms here? Across the hall? Something like that?"

"Yes. They are devoted, of course. But it is often necessary for the Reverend Prentis to withdraw for prayer. For contemplation."

"So," Shapiro said, "you last saw Mr. Prentis walking down the corridor toward his room. He was then in his clerical costume. Clothes, I mean. Did you actually see him go into his room?"

Higgs had not.

"He might, I suppose, have gone into his wife's room, across the hall?"

Higgs did not know. He thought Prentis usually went directly to his own room after a service. "To rest and pray." He might, of course, have gone to his wife's room the night before. "To reassure himself about her health. She was not feeling well yesterday. Otherwise, of course, she would have attended last night's meeting. She is a devoted Christian woman."

"Sick yesterday?"

"Oh, no more than a cold," Higgs said. "She finds this climate difficult, I'm afraid."

"So do I," Shapiro said. "You—I mean the whole—" He paused. Mission? Troupe? He gave it up and said, "Lot of you were going on from here to Chicago?"

"In April we take our mission there," Higgs said. "Were to have taken it there. But now—" He raised narrow shoulders under his black coat. His head did somewhat recede into his collar with the movement. And a kind of blankness came into his eyes.

Shapiro said, "Yes," in a tone of sympathy. He said, "Mr. Prentis was dressed casually when he was killed, as I understand it. In a sports jacket and slacks. Did he often dress that way?"

"At home sometimes, I believe. Never on his ministry. At least, I never saw him dressed that way. A sports jacket and slacks? That is what you said?"

"Yes. The usual question, Mr. Higgs. Did Mr. Prentis have any enemies? Anyone who might—"

"Satan was his enemy," Higgs said. "By all the godly he was loved."

The harsh voice was emphatic, almost peremptory.

It seemed improbable to Shapiro that Satan would have used an ice pick. In any event, Satan was outside his jurisdiction.

"You probably have a good many things to do," he told the Reverend Mr. Higgs. "We'll want to talk to you again, probably."

"My hands will not be idle," Higgs told him.

But they still were when Shapiro went out of the room. Higgs was sitting at the desk. His hands were spread out on the desk. He was looking down at them.

Shapiro turned at the door and looked back at John Wesley Higgs. The emphasis has all gone out of him, Shapiro thought. He seems to have grown smaller. The hands he stares down at have become useless hands, their task completed. More than a man died this morning, Shapiro thought. For this man who is still alive a future died.

5

Shapiro walked down the corridor to have a look at Jonathan Prentis's room. It was already being looked at by Detective (2nd gr.) Carl Maxwell and a man from the precinct squad. Acting Captain Maloney was watching them.

They were laying shirts and handkerchiefs and socks and underwear on one of the twin beds. They were laying clothes from a closet on the other. The clothes were dark and clerical-looking. Shapiro did not see any sports jacket. The one he had been stabbed in, Shapiro thought, must have been the only one he had brought east—the one he had counted on to prevent his being recognized in a public place, or at least in a place no more public than a dimly lighted nightclub in the Village. Where a customer could be even less visible in a booth.

"Sure had a lot of clothes for a man in his trade," Maloney said. "Nothing in any of the pockets we've found so far." He took an envelope out of his jacket pocket. It was sealed and Maloney had written his name and rank and the date on the face of it.

"Six hundred and forty-five dollars in bills under a pile of handkerchiefs," he said. "Hell of a place to leave that much."

Shapiro said, "Yes."

"Get any place with this Higgs?"

"Not especially. That Mrs. Prentis's room?" He gestured toward the door across the hall.

Maloney said, "Yeah," and the door opened and Tony Cook came out and shut it after him. He shrugged his shoulders.

"This Flanders kid is a good kid," he said. "Didn't need any help from me. And didn't get much, probably because there isn't much to get."

What Detective Grace Flanders had got was that Mrs. Prentis had not seen her husband since about six o'clock the evening before. Then she had had dinner with him in her room. On the nights of meetings the Reverend Jonathan Prentis ate very little, and often it was served to both of them in one of their rooms. He had left her about six-thirty and gone to his own room. " 'To pray and prepare himself' is the way she puts it," Tony said. She had taken aspirin. "She's got a pretty bad cold." She had read for a time. "From the Scriptures." Mrs. Mathews had come in at, she thought about eight-thirty to see if she needed anything.

"Mrs. Mathews?" Shapiro said to Maloney.

"Head secretary," Maloney said. "General factotum, way I get it. She's around somewhere. Was, anyway."

If she had been, she would be. People would not have been encouraged to drift away.

"This Mrs. Mathews gave her a sleeping pill," Tony Cook said. "Insisted that she take it, Mrs. Prentis says, 'I knew it was sinful, but I felt so wretched.' " She did not know when she had fallen asleep, but thought it was soon after she had taken the pill. "Nembutal, grain and a half," Tony said. "Mrs. Mathews left the bottle."

Mrs. Prentis had been wakened at a little after eight, by Mrs. Mathews.

"She told me she had bad news," Hope Prentis had told Detective Flanders and, later, Tony Cook. "Dreadful news. That Jonathan had had an accident. That—"

She had broken up then, telling Cook of her wakening.

"She seems to be taking it hard?" Shapiro asked.

"Crying a good deal," Cook said. "Shaking, sort of. Yes, I guess she's had a jolt."

Shapiro raised his eyebrows.

"All right," Tony said. "I wouldn't say she's prostrated, or anything like that. More sort of dazed, maybe." Shapiro waited. "Well," Tony said, "sort of dopey. As if, maybe, she'd taken another sleeping pill before Miss Flanders got there and it had begun to take effect. But that's only guessing."

"She was asleep when her husband came back last night? He didn't—oh, look in to see how she was? Since she was under the weather?"

"If he did, he didn't wake her up. Anyway, that's what she says."

"She has got a cold?"

"Yeah. Sneezing. Runny eyes. I wouldn't say she had pneumonia or anything like that. Head cold. Able to be up and about if she wanted to be up and about." He paused. Then he nodded his head.

"Incidentally," he said, "she's a blonde, Lieutenant. And about thirty, at a guess. A lot younger than the Reverend Prentis was, I'd think."

"He was fifty-one," Shapiro said. "Pretty, Mrs. Prentis?"

"Nobody's pretty with a head cold," Tony said. "But, yes, I'd call her that. She's got on a long-sleeved nightgown that comes up to her chin, pretty near. And she's in bed with a blanket pulled up, so I don't know about the rest of her. But she's got sort of a pretty face, and she's a hell of a lot younger than Prentis was."

"And," Shapiro said, "you don't like her, do you, Tony?"

"Well," Tony said, "call her not my type, Lieutenant."

"Or believe her?"

"Well," Tony said, "there's nothing wrong with the way she tells it. And a grain and a half would put her pretty well out. Particularly if she's not in the habit of taking the stuff. Could have been the way she says."

"Way the book says," Shapiro said, " 'A good detective is always more or less suspicious and very inquisitive.' You might find this Mrs. Mathews, Tony. And be inquisitive. Mr. Higgs will know where she is, probably."

"Room six twenty-three's where she is," Maloney said. "Suppposed to be, anyway."

Tony took two steps down the corridor and then stopped and turned back, because the door to Mrs. Prentis's room opened and a small, trim woman in a dark suit came out into the hall.

"Detective Flanders," Maloney said. "Lieutenant Shapiro, Grace. Homicide."

She repeated Shapiro's name and added, "Sir." She said, "She's gone to sleep. I think she'd taken something just before I went in. Probably the best thing for her to do."

"She's taking it hard, Miss Flanders?" Shapiro asked.

"She's not hysterical, or anything like that. More—sort of dazed. She wanted me to pray with her. That was just before she dozed. I think she wanted me to get down on my knees by the bed."

Grace Flanders spoke dispassionately.

"Did you?"

"I stood still and ducked my head," Detective Flanders said. "I even closed my eyes. When I opened them, she'd gone to sleep."

"Detective Cook's told us what she told you both," Shapiro said. "Did you believe her?"

"No reason not to," Grace Flanders said. "Yes, I guess I did, Lieutenant."

"And," Shapiro said, "that she's fairly young and rather good-looking. In the face, anyway."

"Not all that young," Grace Flanders said. "I'd guess early thirties. As for the rest of her, yes, that's all right the rest of the way. She was coming out of the bathroom when I first went in and she was wearing this long, no-shape nightgown but—well, I wouldn't say there was much the matter with her figure. Tallish, well proportioned. She wants me to ask this Mrs. Mathews to come in. At least, she did just before she went to sleep. Before she asked me to pray with her."

Maloney raised eyebrows at Nathan Shapiro.

"No reason why not," Shapiro said. "Detective Cook's going along to see Mrs. Mathews. Ask her a couple of questions about last night. You may as well go along with him, Miss Flanders."

She said, "Yes, Lieutenant." She said, "Only it's Mrs., by the way."

Shapiro said, "Mrs. Flanders," and watched while she joined Cook and they walked away together down the corridor in search of Room 623.

"Her husband was Peter Flanders," Maloney said. "The one they gave an inspector's funeral to a few years back."

Shapiro remembered. Peter Flanders, detective first grade and off duty, had stopped a car because he recognized one of the four men in it. They recognized him. He had wounded two of the men and killed a third before he was himself killed. The two wounded men were men the police had been looking for for a long time.

"I remember," Shapiro said. "I knew him. He was a good cop."

Cook and Detective Flanders were halfway down the corridor toward the elevators when a tall, broad-shouldered man came toward them and passed them. He had thick yellowish hair. He wore a dark gray suit and a black necktie. When he came up to Shapiro and Maloney, Shapiro saw that gray was creeping into his yellow hair.

He stopped when he reached the two policemen. Slowly, he nodded his head.

"Yes, Captain," he said. He had a low musical voice. "It is the Reverend Prentis." He sighed. "The loss is great," he said. "To our cause. To a world in need of Christ's guidance. The loss is irreparable." He sighed again.

"This is Mr. Farmington, Nate," Maloney said. "He's the choir leader. He volunteered to identify the body, since Mrs. Prentis wasn't up to it. This is Lieutenant Shapiro, Homicide."

Farmington's hand moved as if he were about to reach it out to be shaken. But he did not reach it out. He repeated Shapiro's name. He said, "It is a tragic occasion, Lieutenant."

"Yes," Shapiro said. "You've no doubt it was Mr. Prentis's body? Mr. Higgs felt it couldn't be. Because of the circumstances of his death. Especially, I gathered, the whereabouts of his death."

"It's sure hard to believe," Farmington said. "But there it is, isn't it?"

Shapiro was a little surprised at the lapse into informal speech. He did not express his surprise. He said, "I'm afraid it is, Mr. Farmington."

"In this cheap dive," Farmington said.

"Not cheap," Shapiro said. "Rather an expensive dive. Mr. Higgs thinks he may have gone there as—as part of his missionary work. To convert someone."

"Lead someone to Jesus," Farmington said. "Yeah. It could have been that, I suppose. To save a soul. He was a man of God, Lieutenant."

Shapiro nodded his head in acceptance.

"Of course," Farmington said, "down underneath he was human. The way we all are. He wouldn't have denied it. He, as they say, wrestled with it."

Shapiro repeated the word "they" and inflected a question mark after it.

Farmington shrugged wide shoulders and raised blond eyebrows. The gray hadn't yet crept into the eyebrows. He was a handsome man, Shapiro thought. He was built rather like a football player. One, of course, who was getting along.

"Only," Shapiro said, "that you seemed to disassociate yourself, Mr. Farmington. From 'them.' "

"Didn't mean to," Farmington said. "Different way of putting things, is all. Doesn't mean I'm not a believer. Haven't been saved. Only—I grew up differently. The Reverend Higgs, the Voice himself—well, they use different words. Meaning the same thing, of course."

"You were an opera singer when you were younger, I understand. Before you joined Mr. Prentis's—crusade? Is that what you call it?"

"No. Somebody else has crusades. Ours is a mission, Lieutenant. The Mission of Redemption's the way it's incorporated."

"Incorporated?"

"Yes. Nonprofit religious corporation. Accredited. So contributions are tax-exempt. Not my part of it. My part's the choir."

"Whose part?"

Farmington said he didn't get it.

"The financial setup," Shapiro said. "Who handles it?"

"Oh," Farmington said. "The treasurer. Main office is back in Saint Louis, you know. Man named Henry Pruitt. Stays in Saint Louis mostly. "Mrs. Mathews is the fund chief—assistant treasurer. Travels with us. Signs the checks. That sort of thing."

Shapiro nodded his head. But there was something tickling in his mind. Almost at once he recognized it. It was a name.

"Mrs. Prentis's maiden name was Pruitt, wasn't it?" he said. "Any relation?"

"Brother. Been with us for a good many years. Before I was, matter of fact. Introduced the Voice to his sister years back.

Way I understand it, anyway. As I said, it was before my time."

"You call Mr. Prentis 'the Voice,' " Shapiro said. "Is that—that usage—general? With those in the—" He paused momentarily, and rejected "troupe." He said, "Mission."

"Voice of one crying in the wilderness," Farmington said. "He used that a good deal. Partly that and partly because of his own voice. Actual voice, I mean. Great voice. He could have been a singer." He paused. Then, quickly, he shook his head. "No disrespect," he said. "Wouldn't want you to think that, Lieutenant. He was a man of God. He brought many thousands to Christ." He broke off and looked intently at Shapiro. Then he said, "Shapiro, isn't it?"

"Yes," Shapiro said. "It's a Jewish name, Mr. Farmington. Few more questions I'd like to ask you. Just to get the setup straight in my mind. May want to make a few notes. Some place we could go? Say your room, perhaps?"

"Share a suite with the Reverend Higgs," Farmington said. "There is a living room. Only—well, Higgs may be using it. There're going to be a lot of odds and ends to pull together. It's a big operation, and now the foundation's knocked out from under it."

"Yes," Shapiro said. "If Mr. Higgs needs the living room we can make do in your own room, Mr. Farmington."

Farmington said, "O.K." He said, "Down this way. Right opposite the—"

"I know where it is," Shapiro told him, and they walked down the long corridor. Maloney did not go with them. He said he'd "keep an eye on the boys."

The "boys" would be half a dozen members of the precinct squad he commanded. One of them would be downstairs, trying to check out on the time Farmington had gone to the coffee shop for his cup of coffee the night before; trying to check out the time of the return to the hotel the night before of Higgs and Farmington and the man now dead. Others would be going from room to room on the sixth floor, seeking somebody who had seen Jonathan Prentis leave his room wearing sports jacket and slacks instead of clericals.

Higgs was not in the suite sitting room when Shapiro led the way into it. Shapiro went to sit at the desk. He got a notebook out of his pocket. Witnesses are sometimes impressed when they see things being written down.

He asked Farmington about the night before. He remembered it as Higgs had remembered it—a successful meeting; many had "come forward to accept Christ"; he and Higgs and Prentis had ridden from Madison Square Garden to the hotel in the limousine, which was leased for the time of the mission's appearance in New York. They had got to the hotel a little before eleven. Higgs and the Reverend Prentis had gone up in the elevator.

"You stayed downstairs," Shapiro said. "That's as Mr. Higgs remembers it. For coffee, he says."

That was right.

"For about how long?"

"Half an hour, maybe."

"In the coffee shop, I suppose. It stays open that late?"

"Sure in the coffee shop. Stays open to midnight."

"Were there many other customers in the coffee shop last night, Mr. Farmington?"

"Not very many. You leading up to something, Lieutenant?"

"Just feeling around," Shapiro said. "Trying to get the general shape of last night. You had your coffee. Then you came up here. Went to bed, I suppose?"

"I was tired. Checking the kids in all afternoon. Sometimes some of them fail to show up. Rehearsing them. Sure I went to bed."

"The kids?"

"The choir. Most of them are young. I think of them as kids."

Shapiro said he gathered it was a large choir. He was told that it was around two hundred, half men, half women.

"They all travel with you? You were going on to Chicago from here, I understand. The whole two hundred go along, with the rest of you?"

"I don't see—" Farmington began and Shapiro nodded his head sadly.

"Probably hasn't anything to do with Mr. Prentis's death," Shapiro said. "Start of things, Mr. Farmington, all we can do is sort of bungle around. Try to get the shape, as I said. The choir?"

"Twenty-four regulars go along on the plane," Farmington said. "The Negro quartet plus ten other men and ten women. Sort of help me shape them up, if you know what I mean. The rest I get through their agents. When they've got agents, and most of them have. New York, Chicago, London. All full of hopefuls who want to sing for their suppers. I—well, one way of putting it would be that I sort of order them through their agents. So many sopranos, so many contraltos, so many baritones and tenors."

"Not volunteers, I gather. Er—" He groped for a word. "Not dedicated to the cause."

"We pay scale. The twenty-four regulars get above scale. And I still can't see what this has to do with the Voice's death. Seems to me you'd be working this from the other end, Lieutenant. Starting with this dive he was killed in."

"Oh," Shapiro said, "we're working it from all ends, Mr. Farmington. You'd been in town about how long? I mean, for this mission."

"Three weeks," Farmington said. "Oh, some of us were here earlier, of course. Getting things set up. I was here almost two weeks before we opened. Rounding up the singers. Getting them shaken down. I still don't—"

This time he left it hanging there.

"Because," Shapiro said, "all of you would be, I'd think, in a sense isolated from the city. Living here together. Not, I'd think, meeting too many people outside your own group. I don't say that that narrows it down to members of the group, of course. But—well, it's a place to start. These extra members of the choir. The ones you recruit. I take it they don't live here in the hotel with the rest of you?"

"They live all over town, I guess. Doesn't matter as long as they show up at the Garden. Mrs. Mathews has their names and addresses. So she and her girls can send out the checks."

"Do you suppose Mr. Prentis knew any of these extra boys and girls?"

Farmington shrugged his shoulders. He said he didn't suppose so. He said that the choir—all the details—were left to "people like me." Getting the mission from place to place, leasing the halls in which the meetings were held, handling the press and radio and TV people—all those things were left to people who knew those fields.

"Mr. Prentiss stayed aloof from all that? From the mechanics of the mission?"

"The Reverend Mr. Prentis preached the word of God. His days were filled."

"He preached at these meetings three times a week, as I understand it," Shapiro said. There was no special comment in his tone.

"He spent time in prayer," Farmington said. "Also, there was the syndicated column, of course. Hundreds of papers across the country. And in England, too. Five times a week it appears. And there were television tapes. That sort of thing. To carry the word."

"Mr. Higgs helped with the sermons, he says. With the columns, too?"

"Under the Voice's guidance. With his inspiration. I believe he did. He, too, is a minister of the gospel. A man of God."

At intervals, Shapiro thought, Farmington talks as if he were quoting. But a lot of people do.

"A few minutes ago," Shapiro said, "you said that down underneath, Mr. Prentis was human. Did you mean anything special by that?"

"Nothing. We are all human."

"But," Shapiro said, " 'down underneath'?"

"Nothing," Farmington said. "A—a way of speaking."

Shapiro nodded his head. He said, "Mr. and Mrs. Prentis had been married about ten years, as I understand it. You probably saw a good deal of them."

"Yes."

"From the outside," Shapiro said. "Which is as far as anybody can go, of course. It seemed like a good marriage?"

"I'm sure they were devoted. There was every reason to think they were. Every appearance of devotion. Why do you ask questions like that, Lieutenant?"

"To get the picture," Shapiro said, and made his sad voice

patient. "Apparently he was with a young woman at this restaurant. Before he was killed there. It was not his wife, evidently."

"He was a man of God. If there was a woman with him there was just cause. The cause of God."

"Sure," Shapiro said, pointedly withdrawing from the unctuous; from what sounded like unctuous quotation. "Could have been that way. When you came up last night. After your cup of coffee. You didn't see Mr. Prentis? Perhaps leaving his room? Perhaps in a sports jacket and slacks?"

"I sure as—" Farmington said and stopped himself. He said, "I certainly did not, Lieutenant."

"In the coffee shop when he went out, probably," Shapiro said. "He got to the restaurant downtown about eleven-thirty. Somewhere around then. So he must have have left here shortly after eleven. You'd have been drinking your coffee."

Farmington guessed so.

"With Mr. Prentis dead," Shapiro said, "the—mission will disband? Or will somebody take his place? Perhaps Mr. Higgs?"

Farmington repeated "Higgs?" on a note of evident astonishment. Then he said, "With that voice of his?" Then he shook his head. He said, "Not a chance, Lieutenant. Without the Voice we just—well, I guess we just fold. The work will be in other hands." He sighed. "God's work," he said, in case Shapiro had failed to understand.

"An operation of this size must be—must have been—rather expensive," Shapiro said. "Airplanes. Leases of places like Madison Square Garden. The money came from collections at the meetings? That sort of thing?"

"Some of it, yes. But thousands send contributions to Saint Louis. Many quite large contributions, I've been told. To keep this nation Christian. To turn back the forces of evil. To save the American way of life."

"Very commendable," Shapiro said. "Any idea how much? In a year, say?"

"Our receipts have never been disclosed," Farmington said. "The organization is recognized as a religious community. It is not required—"

"Yes," Shapiro said, "Tax-exempt. Was Mr. Prentis paid a salary?"

"His needs were met," Farmington said. "Listen, I don't know about the financial side of the—the operation. I got paid to manage the music side. I mean, to arrange for voices to be raised in praise."

Sometimes he remembers his lines, Shapiro thought. Sometimes he slips up on them. He almost said he "sure as hell" hadn't seen Prentis leaving the hotel last night. He caught himself. Which didn't need to mean anything about Ralph Farmington, except that he had once been a professional singer and had turned to, or been tossed out to, another profession.

"If you've got to go into the financial setup," Farmington said, "you'll have to ask Mrs. Mathews about it. Or get in touch with Pruitt. Only he's in Saint Louis."

"You told me," Shapiro said. "Probably won't need to. Just trying to get the general picture. You've been very helpful, Mr. Farmington."

His tone was one of dismissal, and Farmington stood up. He started toward the door of his bedroom. Shapiro let him take two steps and then said, "Oh, by the way, Mr. Farmington."

Farmington stopped and turned back.

"The young woman with Mr. Prentis last night," Shapiro said, "seems to have been a blonde. Rather attractive, as the waiter remembers her. Any of the girls in your choir—the ones hired locally or the regulars—fit that description?"

"Pretty vague description," Farmington said. "The regulars, the ones who travel with us, no. Oh, a few blondes. But—well, most of them aren't all that young, Lieutenant. Take the locals, yeah. Maybe a third of the girls, if you stretch the 'attractive.' A few of them, you wouldn't have to stretch it."

"Any particular one come to your mind?"

"No, Lieutenant. I listen to them, see? We don't try to set up a chorus line. Be no point to it anyway, with these surplices they have them wear."

Shapiro nodded his head. Farmington turned and took another step toward the bedroom door and then stopped and turned back again.

"The Reverend Prentis was a man of God," he said, and spoke firmly.

"You told me," Shapiro said, and waited behind the desk while Farmington went into his bedroom and closed the door behind him. Then he went out into the corridor to see how Cook and the others were getting on. He hoped better than he was. He couldn't see that he was getting anywhere at all.

Tony Cook was coming along the corridor. As soon as he saw Shapiro he began to shake his head. Apparently he hadn't been getting anywhere either. Shapiro stopped and waited for him to come up.

"Been going over these singers," Tony said. "Carl and I. Nobody knows anything about anything, except, a couple of them, that now they're out of jobs. And that they got a hundred and fifty a week, plus travel expenses when they were on the road. Last night—"

Last night the twenty-four permanent choir members had come to the hotel from the Garden, arriving at a little before eleven. They had come in a chartered bus. They had gone to the rooms spaced along the central corridor near the end most distant from the two corner rooms occupied by Mr. and Mrs. Prentis. There were twelve of the rooms, each occupied by two men or two women.

And all twenty-four had gone in to their rooms and gone to bed, and each roommate vouched for the other. None had seen the Reverend Mr. Jonathan Prentis after the meeting. None knew until Mrs. Mathews had come to tell them about nine that morning that the Voice had been stilled.

"Way one of them put it," Tony Cook said. "All very proper people. Mostly in their forties. Mostly talk Middle West, or something."

"Any pretty youngish blonde?"

"Like the one at the Brawl? No, Nate. You figure he was a chaser? And, maybe, chased the wrong dame?"

"I don't figure anything at the moment," Shapiro said. "He apparently was with a blonde. And not his wife. Unless—this Mrs. Mathews say she gave Mrs. Prentis a sleeping pill?"

"Yeah," Tony Cook said. "And that's about all she will say.

To me, anyway. She says she'll talk to whoever's in charge, only she won't help anybody pry into what's not their business. What it comes down to, she's damn difficult."

"Has Maloney talked to her? Or any of his boys?"

"Captain Maloney took one look at her and left her to us," Cook said. "Can't say I blame him. But—you'll find out, Nate. In room six twenty-three's where we left her. Mrs. Flanders and I. Up that way."

He gestured up that way.

"You might," Shapiro said, "dig up a man named Acton. In charge of transportation for the troupe. See if he knows anything we ought to know."

"Sure," Cook said and started on along the corridor in the direction he had been going. But after a few steps he stopped and then walked back to Shapiro.

"When you're talking to this Mrs. Mathews," Cook said, "you'd better not smoke. Because I lighted a cigarette in this room of hers, without thinking about it, and got a five-minute lecture. Because, way it seems, smoking's a sin. Against the will of God."

"I can't remember that He mentioned it," Shapiro said. "Nothing about it in the Talmud. Of course, I'm not a scholar."

He went on to Room 623. The door was closed, and he knocked on it. He knocked twice before he was answered, and then it was in a low, rather scratchy, voice. The voice said, "I'm busy."

"Police," Shapiro said through the door. "Like to ask you a few questions, Mrs. Mathews."

"You're this man Maloney? Captain or whatever they call him?"

"No," Shapiro said, and turned the doorknob and pushed the door open.

It opened to a largish room, again evidently the living room of a suite. There was an office desk in the middle of it and a stocky woman sat behind the desk. She had black hair, pulled straight back to a knot behind her head. She also had a slight mustache. She looked at Shapiro through hard black eyes.

"Well," she said, "at least you're not that papist. Who are you?"

Shapiro told her who he was. He said, "Papist, Mrs. Mathews?"

She said, "Well, isn't he? With that name of his?"

"He may be a Roman Catholic," Shapiro said. "I never asked him. Does it matter?"

"Of course it matters. This is a Protestant country. Free to worship God. Free from the Roman yoke. Don't you know that priests of the Catholic Church are permitted to drink intoxicating beverages? Which is a sin against God."

Cook had, Shapiro thought, rather underestimated the difficulty presented by Mrs. Mathews.

"Shapiro," Mrs. Mathews said. "You're Jewish, I take it?"

"Yes," Shapiro said and waited for an explosion. It did not come. Mrs. Mathews said, merely, "I thought so." Then she said, "I am busy. There is much to be done in these tragic hours. What questions do you want to ask me?"

"You gave Mrs. Prentis a sleeping capsule last night," Shapiro said. "That's right, isn't it? Insisted that she take it?"

"She is not well. She needed to sleep. It is not sinful to seek sleep."

"No," Shapiro said. "About what time did you give her this pill?"

It had been about eighty-thirty.

"You left the bottle of capsules with her?"

"Yes. In case she wakened in the night. But at eleven she was sleeping peacefully."

"You went in to make sure?"

"I was concerned about her. She is a true Christian woman. I went to make sure she was well. And, if she wished, to join my prayers with her."

"But you did not waken her?"

"No. As it says in the Scripture, sleep knits up the raveled sleeve of care."

Shapiro had been resisting a good many temptations since he had got to the Hotel Wexley and the evangelical atmosphere. He did not resist this one. He said, "Shakespeare, I think, Mrs. Mathews. Not the Bible."

"I am quite certain it is from Holy Writ," Mrs. Mathews said. "Quite sure. In John, I think. I can look it up if you—"

"Don't bother," Shapiro said. "I've no doubt you're right, Mrs. Mathews. You went to Mrs. Prentis's room. After you had returned from the meeting at the Garden?"

"I did not attend the meeting. I had tasks to perform. Today we were to have continued on our pilgrimage. There were many details to attend to. Business details."

Shapiro said he was sure there had been. She had not seen Mr. Prentis at all during the evening?

She had not.

She had gone to Mrs. Prentis's room that morning to tell her what had happened?

"The Reverend Higgs came to tell me of the tragedy. It was my sad duty to tell Mrs. Prentis."

"A difficult duty," Shapiro said. "She took it hard, of course?"

"She cried out—cried out, 'No! No! *No!*' I prayed with her."

"And, perhaps, suggested she take a sleeping pill? As—sedation?"

"I may have."

"Very wise of you if you did," Shapiro said. "I'll try not to keep you much longer, Mrs. Mathews. A few questions we always have to ask. Did Mr. Prentis have any enemies that you know of?"

"Only the forces of evil. And those who profit from evil."

"And can you think of anyone who gains by his death? In a financial way? Or in any other way?"

"You mean among men? Since Satan profits."

"Yes," Shapiro said. "Among men."

She did not. All Christianity was the loser. All mankind.

"Of course," Shapiro said. "Now I wonder, Mrs. Mathews—"

6

You collect bits and pieces and spread them out and try to shuffle them into a pattern. In his office at a little after one that Thursday afternoon, Nathan Shapiro shuffled and could not see that anything came of it. Or, he morosely thought, ever would.

There were a few more pieces by the afternoon, few of which Shapiro had collected on his own.

Mrs. Florence Mathews had refused to discuss the financial setup of the Mission of Redemption, Inc. She was not authorized to discuss it. It could not have anything to do with the death of Jonathan Prentis, minister of the gospel. Hence, it was none of the business of the New York police. In any event, she was not authorized. Mr. Pruitt—Mr. Henry Pruitt, treasurer of the Mission of Redemption, Inc.—might divulge what he chose. Mr. Pruitt remained in St. Louis.

The St. Louis police were cooperating. They had, so far, verified that the headquarters of the Mission were in St. Louis. They had established that the Reverend Jonathan Prentis had been president and the Reverend John Wesley Higgs vice-president and Henry Pruitt, a mere "Mr.," treasurer. Mr. Pruitt had not reached his office when the police reached it. His secretary did not know when, under the circumstances—the *dreadful* circumstances—he might be expected. Nobody else was authorized to give any information.

The office was reasonably large and well equipped. It was not very extensively occupied when the St. Louis police visited it. Everybody of importance, except Mr. Pruitt himself, was with the Voice in New York. Or, of course, had been. Yes, that was what the Reverend Mr. Prentis was called—"the Voice." Had been called. When meetings were being held away from town, there were only enough people in the office to handle the mail. Yes, the mail was heavy. The mail was always heavy. Yes, many contributions did come by mail. But they would have to ask Mr. Pruitt himself about that. When he came in. If he came in. He might have decided it would be necessary for him to fly to New York.

Bits and pieces. Bits and pieces. And no pattern to them.

There had been two waiters in the coffee shop of the Hotel Wexley the night before. They were the night men and had to be found and waked up. Both knew Mr. Ralph Farmington by sight. He had been at the hotel for a good many weeks and had often dropped in late for coffee. Last night? Neither was sure about last night. Maybe he had come in and maybe he hadn't. If he said he had, they guessed he had. He was a religious man. The whole hotel was full of religious people. It was sure too bad about the Reverend Prentis.

There was a bar at the hotel. The night bartender—who also had to be found and waked up—had never, so far as he knew, seen any Mr. Farmington. Of course, he didn't ask customers their names. Their names were none of his business. If this Mr. Farmington was one of that crowd on the sixth floor, he couldn't see him coming in for a drink. Talked like the stuff was poison, that crowd did.

There were several bars within a few blocks of the hotel and a few places where a thirsty man might get coffee. A couple of detectives were going from place to place, at first with only a verbal description of Ralph Farmington; later, when his former agents—Talent, Incorporated—had been located, with photographs. But the photographs had been taken ten years earlier, when Farmington's blond hair had had no gray in it. And had, as it turned out, been longer. Nobody recognized the photograph.

Copies of the photograph had gone downtown and then, as they were rounded up—waked up—been shown to waiters and bus boys and the hat-check girl at the Village Brawl. Nobody remembered seeing anybody who looked like that.

None of the waiters remembered seeing anything else the night before, except a lot of customers. Nobody saw anybody stick an ice pick into anybody. Emile Schmidt, who had the station nearest Booth 22, remembered giving André a hand up and taking two drinks to the booth. Sure there was a girl there. Yes, she was a blonde. Yeah—m'sieu—she was what you'd call good-looking. Maybe he'd know her if he saw her again and maybe he wouldn't. Sure, if a girl who looked like her came in and he happened to notice he'd give the police a ring.

Jonathan Prentis had been a well-nourished male in, probably, his early fifties. Cause of death, a stab wound which had penetrated the heart, slightly nicking a rib in the course of entry. The wound was consonant with one which might have been inflicted by the purported weapon. There had been extensive internal bleeding and probably very quick loss of consciousness. Analysis revealed 0.17 per cent of alcohol in the blood, which might have produced mild clinical symptoms of intoxication. In some men, but not necessarily in others. Tests to determine the alcoholic content of the brain and other organs were proceeding. Post-mortem examination had revealed no anatomical abnormalities except for a slightly enlarged thyroid gland.

Adele Lorraine, the singer with the combo, had been located and waked up—and had been pretty sore about it. She had seen nothing unusual the night before from the low stage she stood on to sing. The usual mob out front. Talking through her songs, like always. If she'd seen a tall dark man in Booth 22 she hadn't paid any attention to him and why for God's sake should she? She sure as hell hadn't seen anybody stick an ice pick into him. An ice pick, for God's sake!

The ice pick had a shaft four and a half inches long, which had been long enough. The octagonal wooden handle had been of the same length and three inches in circumference. The pick apparently was fairly new and had been inexpensive. The wooden handle revealed no identifiable fingerprints—only a few smudges. Hardware stores in the neighborhood of the Village Brawl were being checked, but with no special optimism. There was little demand nowadays for ice picks, which was a plus factor. The ice pick in question was indistinguishable from thousands of others and might have been bought anywhere in the city. Or, for that matter, in any city. Which was a minus factor.

The four elevators at the Hotel Wexley were automatic. The

doorman went off at nine o'clock at night. The desk, which was staffed twenty-four hours a day, was set so that it did not command a view of the elevators or of most of the stretch of lobby between them and the door.

The night clerk, wakened in his small room on the hotel's top floor—and not at all pleased about it—did remember that Higgs and Prentis had picked up their keys at a little before eleven. Or maybe ten-thirty. Or he thought he remembered it. He didn't remember anything about Farmington. Sure, Higgs's key would unlock the door to the suite he and Farmington shared. So Farmington wouldn't have needed to ask for his duplicate to get in. Provided, Shapiro had thought, he didn't mind waking Higgs. Also, there was this—a lot of guests just put hotel keys in their pockets, instead of leaving them at the desk. No, he hadn't seen Farmington in the lobby after the others had gone up. If they had gone up. No, he couldn't see the entrance of the coffee shop from his spot at the desk. And it wasn't his job to keep a check on the guests. And it was a hell of a time to wake a man up.

Bits and pieces without discernible pattern. To me, Shapiro thought. Probably plain as day to somebody else. Somebody cut out for this sort of thing.

Somebody knocked at the door of Shapiro's small office and Shapiro said, "Yeah?" in a dispirited way, and Anthony Cook came in.

"Gave this girl who sings—sang—in the choir another ring," Tony said. "This Janet Rushton. No soap. Also, I finally ran down this guy Acton. Who handles transportation for them. He was canceling an airplane. Charter. Supposed to take off from Kennedy at one o'clock today. Seems the airline's a little stuffy about it. Canceling, I mean. Got the airplane all fueled up and panting to go."

Tony sat down in response to Shapiro's gesture and lighted a cigarette. The smoke from it eddied toward Nathan Shapiro, who is trying to cut down. Tony reached the pack toward him, with a cigarette protruding. "You're sure a help," Nathan told him, and took the cigarette. He said, "Get anything from Acton?"

Tony couldn't see that he had. However, for what it was worth—

Most of those who made up the mission had reached New York on March second, by chartered flight from St. Louis. That had been a Monday. The first gospel meeting had been on the following Wednesday. On that flight had been the permanent members of the choir, including the Negro quartet, Mrs. Mathews and Mrs. Prentis, Mrs. Mathews's three assistants and a man named Laurence Petty, who was, so far as Tony Cook could make out, a stage manager. There were also other technicians—the lighting engineer, the man who supervised the sound, a camera crew of three. The chartered jet had also taken to Kennedy the personal luggage of all concerned, cartons filled with robes for the choir and the cross which served as a backdrop.

"Hell of a big thing, that cross," Tony said. "But it breaks down into sections."

Acton had met the plane with a leased limousine for Mrs. Mathews and Mrs. Prentis and any others who could be got into it and a chartered bus for the rest and had taken them all to the Hotel Wexley and their rooms on the sixth floor. The cartons of robes—"Hell of a lot of them for that big an outfit" —and the sectioned cross had been trucked to the Garden, where the first meeting had been held the following Wednesday.

"March fourth, that was," Tony said, pinning it down. "They couldn't get into the Garden until that morning. Prize fight the night before."

It had all gone smoothly, according to Theodore Acton. "He sounds like being a pro. Is, I guess. One time he was a transportation officer for the navy, turns out. Knows his business. Didn't mention God the whole time I talked to him."

"Made a change," Shapiro said. "He'd come on ahead, I gather? You say he met the others at the airport."

"He came on February twentieth to set things up," Tony Cook said and reached out to a tray to crush out his cigarette. Nathan Shapiro was nursing his.

"He and a man named Gerald Humphrey," Tony Cook said.

"Humphrey's what Acton calls 'the man who makes contact with the communications media.' Which, I guess, means press agent."

"That's their usual M.O.?"

"Yes, according to Acton. The advance guard usually gets to the place they're having the meetings a week or two ahead. It's quite an operation."

"Was," Nathan said. "Nothing unusual about the operation this time?"

Tony lighted another cigarette. He drew on it and looked at the glowing coal and said, "Well," drawing it out a little.

"Nothing specially unusual, according to Acton," he said. "Prentis himself came along with the advance party. Sometimes he did and sometimes he didn't. And the Reverend Higgs came along too. Usually he didn't. Stayed behind and came along with the main party. But sometimes he did. Way Acton put it, 'if he was caught up.' "

Nathan Shapiro repeated the last two words.

"Yes," Tony said. "I asked him what he meant and he looked sort of surprised and, it seemed to me, as if he wished he hadn't said it. Then he said, 'Getting out the syndicate column and the magazine articles and that sort of thing. He does a lot of editing for the Voice.' "

"Editing?"

"I quote," Tony said and took a deep drag. Nathan sighed and stubbed out his own cigarette. The smoke from Tony's still smelled good. "I wondered too, Nate."

"A ghost," Shapiro said. "Does sound like that, doesn't it? Higgs himself didn't come out with it, but I wondered then. The four of them—Prentis and Higgs and this man Humphrey and Acton. They all moved into the Wexley. Where they are now?"

"Not on the same floor," Tony said. "That wasn't cleared for them until the second. Humphrey and Acton and Higgs had rooms there, yes. But Prentis didn't. He stayed downtown. At the Fifth Avenue Hotel. It's in the Village. Few blocks from this Village Brawl place, actually. Big old hotel. A lot of permanent residents. Some of them have been there for years, way they look. A—oh, a sedate sort of place. Except recently quite a few boys and girls from N.Y.U. seem to have moved in. Still a very respectable place. Better class than the Wexley."

He was told he seemed to know it.

"There's a bar we—I mean I—drop into now and then. Called the Amen Corner. And last summer they had a sidewalk cafe."

It would, Nathan thought, be another place to put on his list of telephone numbers to try when in search of Detective Anthony Cook. He said, "Acton have any idea why the Reverend Prentis went downtown to this hotel?"

"He said, 'He was a very conscientious man. It would be like him.' "

Nathan raised both shoulders and eyebrows.

"Yeah," Tony said. "I wondered too. Seems the Reverend hadn't saved New York for a couple of years. And likes to be up-to-date on a city's wicked spots. So, he picked the Village. Hippies and yippies and boys with long hair. Most of them are over in what they call the East Village."

"Used to be just the lower east side," Shapiro said. "But there are specimens on Eighth Street, of course. Just a block from the Fifth Avenue Hotel."

Tony Cook said he would say there were. But then, momentarily, he looked over Nathan Shapiro's head. Then, rather slowly, he said, "Only—" and let it hang. Shapiro waited.

"At this meeting we went to last night," Tony said. "This meeting of his. They had a movie to show how wicked New York is. But it wasn't a movie about the wickedness of Greenwich Village. It was about Forty-second Street. You know the blocks there."

Nathan knew the blocks.

"Of course," Tony said, "he may have given the Village a going-over at one of the other meetings."

"Sure," Shapiro said. "There's enough wickedness to go around. Did he make these—these tours of inspection in other cities they saved? London? Los Angeles? Chicago?"

"Sometimes, Acton says. If he hadn't visited them recently."

"Had he planned to inspect Chicago before they opened there?"

"Not that Acton knows of. He'd booked Mr. and Mrs. Prentis to Little Rock, which is where they've got a house."

Nathan said, "Mmmm." He said, "Mrs. Prentis came east this time with the others. On the charter flight?"

"Yeah. According to Acton, anyway. Flew up from Little Rock to Saint Louis the Saturday before they all came along here. She won't fly on Sunday. Thinks it's a profanation or something."

Shapiro said, "Mmmm." He said, "This motion picture at the meeting last night. All about Forty-second Street?"

"Yeah."

"Not canned stuff? I mean, old news shots? That sort of thing?"

"Looked pretty recent. He did have a cameraman of his own. Man named—" Tony got a notebook out of his pocket and found a name. "Named Marvin Resnik. And a couple of assistants."

Shapiro said, "Mmmm," again. He said, "No shots of the Village?"

"Not last night, anyway. Could be he didn't find the kind of wickedness that would make a good picture."

For some seconds, Shapiro looked at Tony Cook, apparently without seeing him. Tony started to get up. He had a report to type out. If he had become invisible to Nate, he might as well, he thought, get on with the chore. It was a chore he didn't like.

"Tell you," Shapiro said, "maybe you'd better go down to this Fifth Avenue Hotel. Dig around a little. Two weeks away from the others, if it was that way, he'd have had a chance to make contacts. We might widen things out a bit." He sighed. Things were wide enough already, and vague enough.

Tony stood up. He said, "O.K., Nate." He started out of the office.

"Trouble is," Shapiro said, "Now all the people we've been talking to—all those connected with this mission of Prentis's—stand to lose. Because the mission falls apart and, religious or not, they've got livings to make. If we can find somebody outside it might help."

Tony said, "Yeah," again and that he saw what Shapiro meant.

When he had gone, Shapiro swung his typewriter in front of him. He ran forms into it and filled in a few spaces. Then he looked at the sheets sadly. Reports have to be typed out, according to regulations. But there is little point in typing on fog. He swung the typewriter away again and took up his telephone and asked to be connected with Captain William Weigand. The operator said, "Sorry, Lieutenant. The captain's in court. On the Peridenti one."

Angelo Peridenti was on trial for the murder of a former associate in a trucking corporation. The police were sure, but Peridenti had a lot of money and, hence, a lot of lawyers.

Shapiro went downstairs and got a car and said, "Up to the Wexley," to the driver.

Tony Cook went downtown by subway. It wasn't raining quite as hard as it had been, and when he walked from the Sheridan Square station east to the Fifth Avenue Hotel the wind was behind him. Which put the wind from west or northwest; a clearing wind. It hadn't got around to clearing yet, but it would. By evening, they'd be able to walk to the movie on dry sidewalks. If she really held out for the movie.

The Fifth Avenue Hotel is massive. It has been at the corner of Fifth Avenue and Ninth Street for a long time. You can go into it from Ninth Street and come into the big lobby near the desk. You can look across the lobby at a spreading dining room, and one evening when Tony had stopped in the bar, which is on the Fifth Avenue side, there had been a big party in the dining room, with an orchestra and dancing. A wedding reception, he had thought it was.

A pleasant woman at the desk said, "Last month? I don't know. We're jam-packed. We have been all winter." She looked at the picture of Jonathan Prentis. She shook her head. She said, "There're so many of them, Mr. Cook. Coming and going."

She went into a small office behind the desk and came out with a middle-aged and immaculate man. "The resident manager, Mr. Cook," she said. "Perhaps he can help you with your problem." She said, "Yes, Mr. Williams," to a man standing behind Cook. "You have a reservation. If you'll just sign—"

Tony moved aside out of the way. There was a couple behind Mr. Williams, with luggage surrounding them.

"Mrs. Gaines says you're a detective," the resident manager said. "Inquiring about a former guest of ours?"

Tony said, "Yes," and took his badge out of his pocket and showed it. The resident manager looked at it and said, "Ah," and then, "Perhaps we'd better step into the office. Door at the end of the desk." He pointed to the door he meant and, when Tony Cook took the few steps to it, opened the door for him. Inside, the resident manager sat behind a desk and motioned Tony to a chair and said, "Now this guest, Mr. Cook?"

Tony repeated what he had told the woman who appeared to be Mrs. Gaines. He said, "A man named Jonathan Prentis. Supposed to have checked in late last month. Probably on the twentieth."

"We'll have to check our—" the resident manager said and then, with emphasis, "Jonathan *Prentis?* The man who—" He did not finish but shook his head instead.

"Yes," Cook said. "The same man."

"A tragic thing," the resident manager said. "A great man. A dedicated man. Quite near here it happened, wasn't it? A—er—place called the Village Brawl. But that was only last night. You're asking about last month."

"He may have been in this part of town then," Tony said. "Probably nothing to do with his death. But we have to check things out. If you would have a look at—"

"Of course," the resident manager said. "Of course, Mr. Cook."

He used the telephone. He kept on using it for other purposes while Tony waited. A young woman with a very short skirt came in and put papers on the desk. The resident manager said, "Here we are," and then, "Maybe you'll want to look at it yourself, Mr. Cook," and reached the papers across the desk to Tony.

The one on top, clipped to the one under it, was a typed letter, on a letterhead which read, "Mission of Redemption, Inc.," with a St. Louis, Missouri, address printed under it. The letter, written on February 14 from St. Louis, requested the reservation of a single room from February 20 to March 2 for Mr.

Jonathan Prentis—a single room with bath, preferably an inside room away from traffic. The letter was signed "T. S. Acton." At the bottom of the letter somebody had written, with a ballpoint, "Conf. 2/18. ltr & phone."

The letter was clipped to a receipted bill. Jonathan Prentis had checked in on February 20 and out again on March 2. He had had Room 1106 and had paid twenty-two dollars a day for it. Plus tax. He had been charged with several telephone calls marked "Local" and with one "Lg. Dis." to Little Rock, Arkansas. The number to which that call had been made was typed in, and Tony copied it down.

The resident manager finished talking on the telephone and Tony slid the receipted bill and the letter back across the desk. He said, "Doesn't seem to have eaten here. Unless he paid cash, of course."

"The restaurant and the hotel operate separately," the resi dent manager said. "Actually, the restaurant is a concession. They will charge through us, but they prefer to be paid direct."

"You don't remember Mr. Prentis yourself?" Tony asked him. "Tall, dark man. Rather good-looking. Dressed like a priest. Most of the time, anyway."

The resident manager shook his head. He said, "There are so many, Mr. Cook. Coming and going so rapidly. Unless there is —unless something special comes up, I'm not likely to remember individuals. Some—er—complaint about service. Yes, that might come to me. But we have very few complaints here. In clerical garb, you say?"

"Yes. Part of the time, anyway."

"But many of the clergy stay with us," the resident manager said. "Are confident that this is—call it a respectable place to stay. A quiet place, if you know what I mean."

Tony said he did.

"No—er—boisterous parties," the resident manager said. "We discourage that sort of thing."

Tony said he was sure they did. He said that, if there were no objections, he'd ask around a little to see if any of the staff remembered Mr. Prentis.

"Of course," the resident manager said, and lifted a telephone which was ringing at him. "By all means, Mr. Cook."

A bellman in uniform was sitting on a bench opposite the desk. He came promptly to his feet when Cook stopped in front of him, came with a smile and said, "Sir?" But he did not remember, especially, a talk dark man, possibly dressed like a priest. That didn't mean he hadn't seen him. It meant that February twentieth was a long time ago and there were lots of tall dark men—and short light men—in between. He'd ask the other guys. He'd be glad to. If he found one who remembered he'd—what should he do?

He should call the local police precinct and say he had a message for Detective Cook. If one of the other bellmen remembered a Reverend Mr. Jonathan Prentis and anything—well, anything special—about him. The bellman said, "Yes, sir."

Cook went through the big lobby and turned left and went into the bar, which was also a café. It was by then almost four in the afternoon, and the tables were empty. But there was a man sitting at the end of the bar with a drink in front of him. He was reading the New York *Post* over his drink. There was a man behind the bar, polishing glasses in an unhurried sort of way. He put down the glass he was polishing when Tony pulled a stool out and sat on it. He said, "Yes, sir?"

It was early for it, but Tony said, "Bourbon on the rocks. Old Fitzgerald." He didn't for a moment know why he had specified a brand, and then he remembered that Old Fitzgerald was what somebody had been drinking the night before at the Village Brawl. With ginger ale, for God's sake.

When the drink was in front of him, he got out the photograph of Jonathan Prentis. He said, "Ever see this man? He apparently was here at the hotel a while back. Remember whether he ever dropped in here?"

The barman said, "Huh?" and Tony showed him the badge.

The barman looked at the picture and shook his head and said, "Wanted for something? People who come in here are respectable people. People like professors from N.Y.U."

"Not wanted for anything," Tony Cook said. "He's dead. Murdered a few blocks from here. Man named Prentis."

The barman looked again at the picture and shook his head again and said, "Nope. Don't remember him." Then he said, "Hey! That evangelist fellow?"

"Yes."

"Wouldn't be coming to the bar, would he? That type are down on the stuff, way I get it."

"He might have come in for lunch or dinner," Tony said. "Hard to find a place to eat around here where you can't buy a drink."

"Sure as hell is," the barman said.

"He might have been wearing clericals," Tony said. "Dressed like a priest."

"We get priests, all right," the barman said. "There's Father O'Malley. Comes in for dinner two-three times a week. Drinks Soave. Italian wine, that is. We keep it chilled for him. But he's got red hair, what there is of it. Not like this guy."

Witnesses wander. A detective grows used to it.

"Any of the waiters around?" Cook asked. He was told, hell, no. Not in the middle of the afternoon. Anybody who might remember whether the Reverend Mr. Prentis had been in the café, or for that matter the big restaurant beyond it, for meals between, say, the twentieth of February and the second of March? And, of course, whether he had had anybody with him? Which was the point of it, if there was any point to it.

The boss, maybe. He was out there.

Out there was through a doorway and down two steps into the main dining room. The boss was sitting at a table against a pillar. He had oblongs of paper in front of him and he was looking at them and now and then putting his initials on one of them and laying that one aside. He had a glass of wine ready to his left hand, out of the way of the pencil in his right. He was Henri, with, apparently, no last name. Yes, he was the maître d'.

He looked at the picture of Jonathan Prentis and shook his head. He didn't remember having seen a man who looked like that in the café or in the restaurant. But he saw, and seated, a lot of people. Late last month to early this? That was a long time. A Reverend Mr. Prentis who had been killed the night before in a place called the Village Brawl? That was too bad. He understood that Granzo had quite a thing going at the Brawl. Building it up, they said Granzo was.

Room-service waiters?

Room service was handled out of the dining room. There wasn't a great deal of it. A few breakfasts. "A good many of the rooms have kitchen facilities," Henri said. "That way when we took over. Permanents pretty much get their own breakfasts. Have to bring in their own utensils—coffeepots, that sort of thing—but there's no way to stop them doing it. We do send up some breakfasts."

The waiters who took up breakfasts?

Couple of men did most of that unless there was a rush, which mostly there wasn't. On account of these damn kitchen facilities. Max Hansen. Ricardo Florez. Florez was married and lived over in Queens. Hansen had a room at the hotel. One of the rooms over the kitchen. Yes, he might be in it. He didn't go on until six. In the morning? In the morning, he went on at seven. Sure he was off during the lunch hour.

"Sorry I can't help you more," Henri said, and went back to checking out the lunch business and sipping his wine.

The bellhop with the smile was still on the bench across from the desk. Or, of course, was back on it. Sure he knew where Maxie's room was. Sure, he'd show Mr. Cook.

Max Hansen's room was at the end of a long corridor on the second floor, and twenty-five cents away from Tony Cook's pocket—twenty-five cents which he wouldn't get back, except as a beaming smile and a "Thank you, sir," as if it had been a dollar.

Max Hansen's room was small, and it was certainly over the kitchen. Tony could hear the kitchen under it and smell the kitchen in it, because the single window on an air shaft was partly open. Max Hansen was small and almost completely bald, and he wore dark trousers and a white shirt open at the neck and very clean. He was reading a paperback book, and the title was in a language which looked a little like German, but not quite like it. Swedish, Tony guessed. Tony was sorry to barge in, but—

Max Hansen looked at the picture and said. "Sure. Eleven-oh-six. One egg, soft-boiled, and toast and Sanka. Seven-thirty on the dot every morning. Paid cash, like the boss wants them to. Always had change after the first morning. Always gave me a quarter. Which was ten per cent, but what the hell? It takes all kinds."

When had this been?

Sometime late last month. Yes, the twentieth to the second would be about right. No, there wasn't anything in particular to remember about Mr.—what was the name again? Oh, sure, Mr. Prentis. Just a nice-enough guy who always was up when his breakfast came and always said "Good morning" and had the change ready. Up and dressed? Yes. Partly dressed, anyway. Dark trousers and a white shirt. Collar attached to shirt?

"Now you mention it, mister, no. No collar on the shirt—open at the neck, as I remember. Make a difference?"

"Sometimes," Tony told him, "Mr. Prentis wore clericals. Like a priest. Have to button the collars on separately. At least, I suppose they do."

Max Hansen shook his head. He didn't know—just thought it was that kind of shirt.

"Anything else you do remember?" Tony asked him. "I know it was a good while ago and that you take a lot of breakfasts up. Anything at all? I mean, he was always up and had trousers and shirt on. Never—well, never any sign of a hangover? Anything like that?"

"No. Nice clean gentleman. Always shaved, which mostly they aren't at that time in the morning. Smelled of after-shave lotion part of the time. Nice clean old boy."

Hansen had been sitting on a chair with its back to the window, Tony Cook on a straight desk chair. Tony got up from his chair and said, "Thanks, Mr. Hansen. Sorry to have barged in on your rest time."

Max Hansen stood up too. He was a little heavy, but he had quick, neat movements.

Tony Cook reached for the doorknob, which he could do without moving, so small was the room. He stopped with his hand on the knob and turned back.

He said, "This after-shave lotion you smelled. Sure it was that, Mr. Hansen?"

Hansen shrugged his shoulders. He said, "What else?"

"Not a woman's perfume?"

"The maids aren't supposed—" Hansen said and stopped. He said, "I see what you mean. No, I wouldn't think so. Not that kind of a man, from what I saw of him. Anyway, this isn't that kind of hotel, mister."

"Any man can be that kind of man," Tony said. "And any hotel—well, no hotel can make people moral. And this one, like most nowadays, has elevators people operate themselves. And I imagine there aren't too many people in the lobby late at night."

"No. Our guests turn in early, mostly. But I still think Mr. Prentis wasn't that kind of man. Didn't you say he was a clergyman or something?"

"Yes. It could have been a woman's perfume? This after-shave lotion."

"Well," Hansen said, "Along about then I had a cold, sort of. Nasty weather we were having."

"Yes," Tony said. "It sure was, Mr. Hansen. This room eleven-oh-six. One bed in it, or two?"

"Single room," Hansen said. "Double bed." He suddenly snapped his fingers. "I remember now," he said. "When I'd bring his breakfast up, the bed was always smoothed out. Not made up, you know what I mean. Just spread up, sorta."

7

Tony couldn't see that he had very much. He couldn't see that he had anything. The Reverend Mr. Jonathan Prentis had stayed a couple of weeks at the Fifth Avenue Hotel. He had Room 1106 and had paid twenty-two dollars a day for it. He had been a neat man who used after-shave lotion and spread his bed up before the waiter brought his breakfast, which consisted of one soft-boiled egg and toast and Sanka. He had had breakfast every morning at seven-thirty, which, presumably, meant that his search for wickedness in Greenwich Village had not required late hours, when wickedness might be most expected to prevail. No photographer named Marvin Resnik had been registered at the hotel at the same time. (Tony had had to make a return trip to the desk to check that out.)

It wasn't raining when Tony went out of the hotel into Fifth Avenue. When he crossed Ninth Street, walking toward the Square, the wind was brisk through it from the northwest, and the sky that way was beginning to brighten. It would be cold tonight, but it wouldn't be raining.

It's as short a way as any other to the subway, Tony thought, and walked along Washington Square, against the wind, and turned to his left and then to his right and found the number he was looking for in Washington Place. It was the number of a three-story brick building with half a dozen worn sandstone steps leading up to a doorway. Rather a good doorway, Tony thought. The house was one which had once, a good many years ago, been a private house. It would be converted to apartments now—floor through, perhaps. Perhaps two to a floor.

Four name slots on the wall in the entry hall. Four mailboxes and four bell buttons. Basement apartment, apparently. It would be at garden level. "Janet Rushton" on the top floor. Only her name in the slot. Tony rang the doorbell above her name. He rang it twice, like a postman. He waited to be spoken to through the grill above the button and was not. Nor did the inner door of the entry hall clatter at him. He tried again, after giving Janet Rushton time to finish whatever she was doing. Nothing came of that. He looked through the grill of her mailbox. She hadn't picked up her mail.

It didn't matter. It was a hundred to one that she would have nothing to tell them. Probably it was a thousand to one. She might, conceivably, be a peephole into the Mission of Re-emption, Inc.—a peephole from outside. He'd give her another ring later.

He went down the sandstone steps and walked west, across Sixth Avenue, and on to Sheridan Square. He rode up to Twenty-third on a local and walked down to West Twentieth and up stairs to the squad room of Homicide South. He checked on Lieutenant Nathan Shapiro and found he wasn't in his office and typed out his own report. He finished it at five o'clock and checked out and took a taxi home, since he had a date at six-thirty—a date which required a second shave and a shower and a suit just back from the cleaners.

Nathan Shapiro climbed familiar stairs out of a subway station in Brooklyn and walked familiar streets. He stopped to buy the latest edition of the New York *Post* ("Evangelist Slain! Story on Page 3.")

Cleo heard his footfalls on the staircase and barked excitement and jumped against the door to hurry him. Which meant, by the pattern of the little Scotty's behavior, that Rose wasn't home yet and that Cleo was lonely. And, of course, starving. And probably wanted to go out for a walk.

Shapiro let himself in and, when Cleo jumped up to him, caught her and held her in his arms for a moment and told her that she was a good dog and that he would feed her as soon as he got his raincoat off. He got his raincoat off and hung it in the closet, and Cleo spoke sharply from the kitchen, wanting to know what was keeping him from a matter of utmost importance. He fed Cleo, who ate eagerly and didn't say anything, after she had finished, about going out. Which, Nathan thought, was just as well. He took his jacket off and unstrapped his gun and put it on its shelf and put his jacket back on again and sat in front of the fireplace, which was only an electric heater, whatever its pretense. He looked at the portrait of his father over the fireplace. He felt that Rabbi Emmanuel Shapiro was looking down at him. Probably with disappointment.

He would be justified, Nathan thought. I'm out of my depth, as always. As always, I'm the wrong man for the job Bill Weigand's given me. These are people I am incapable of understanding; people who are alien to me as I am to them. It is not that their faith is different from my faith. I am not one of those Jews who must always remember his Jewishness. As many of our friends are Christians as are Jews. No issue arises.

But these people are violent in their belief. Their religious belief is like a rushing wind on which they ride and with which they buffet. I am incapable of understanding people like these —like Higgs and this Mrs. Mathews, who thinks that the smoke from a cigarette is the smoke from hell. Quite literally, probably. Not a pallid thing like a hazard to your health. A sinful thing.

Nathan Shapiro lighted a cigarette and wished Rose would come home. Rose sustains him. He got up from the sofa in front of the fireplace and turned on all the lights in the living room. Although it was not cold in the room, he switched on the electric element in the fireplace. It was not cold, but he felt the dreariness of cold.

The afternoon had got him nowhere. The Reverend Higgs had, of course, known that Prentis, that the Voice, had come east earlier than the others and had stayed downtown at the Fifth Avenue Hotel, not at the Wexley with himself and Acton and Farmington and Humphrey. There was nothing unusual about it. He often came early to the scene of their meetings; came to "prepare himself." Came to seek out sin that he might destroy it; came to withdraw himself in prayer. Yes, it was not unusual for him to go alone. "Into the wilderness." That had seemed to Shapiro an unusual way to describe the kind of hotel Tony Cook said the Fifth Avenue was, but Higgs and the others spoke an unusual language.

Higgs had not visited the Voice at the downtown hotel. He had devoted himself to his duties. "Did my little for the cause we serve." He supposed that Prentis might have made contacts —"with the unsaved"—during his week of preparing himself. He knew nothing of that.

Theodore Acton had made Prentis's reservation at the Fifth Avenue and taken him there in the rented limousine and made sure that the room was ready. On March second, after the chartered plane had arrived, he had sent the car down to bring Prentis to the Wexley. Yes, Mrs. Prentis had come with the main body. She usually did. Acton had not seen Prentis during the ten days before the meetings began at the Garden.

Neither had Farmington. Farmington had been busy getting his choir together and into shape.

Marvin Resnik, the photographer, had spent his time shooting pictures of sinful places. Forty-second Street. Sure. The Bowery. Some shots of Harlem and some in the East Bronx. Nothing in Greenwich Village. He hadn't known that the Voice was staying at the Fifth Avenue Hotel. He knew what was wanted without being told. He'd made, maybe, a dozen films. They didn't use the same one at every gospel meeting.

It had been a wasted afternoon. It had, in fact, been a wasted day. He—

Rose's key scraped in the lock. He walked across the room to meet her, and she looked up at him and said, "You're tired, Nathan. Have you had your wine? I'm sorry I'm late, dear."

He bent down to kiss her and, as their lips met, relaxation ran through his mind. He sighed his relaxation, and she pushed him a little way from her and looked up at him. She looked at him for seconds. She said, "You're very tired, Nathan. They make you work too hard and start your work too early on a rainy morning."

He smiled down at her. He said, "Yes, tired, I suppose. And out of my depth, Rose. Way out of my depth."

She smiled, too. There was gentle amusement in her smile. She said, "Of course you are, Nathan. Or think you are. Sit down and I'll get us drinks."

She watched him, obedient, go back to the sofa in front of the fireplace. She started toward the kitchen and he said, "I think

I'll have a Scotch and water tonight. A very small Scotch and water."

She stopped in surprise and turned to look at him. She said, "Of course, darling," and went on, thinking that it must have indeed been a very bad day. He looked at the glowing coils in the fireplace and looked up at the portrait of his father. He thought, "I'm sorry, Papa," and heard the clatter of ice as Rose stirred her martini. She brought their drinks in on a tray and put the tray down on the table between sofa and fireplace. They lifted drinks.

"People I don't understand," he said. "People I'll never understand, Rose."

"I know," Rose said. "It was in the paper. And you told me a little this morning. Evangelists are hard to understand. I realize that. The prophets must have been, dear. They're people, like all of us. You have great understanding of people."

She raised her glass to the portrait of Rabbi Emmanuel Shapiro. She said, "As your father had."

Always, Nathan Shapiro thought, she tries to buoy me up. Always she refuses to accept what is obviously true. He took a sip from his glass. His stomach probably was going to be very annoyed.

"Painters you didn't understand," she said. "And another time it was theater people you couldn't understand. And both times you understood in the end. Don't you remember that, darling?"

"It was luck," he said. "I bungle into things sometimes. I suppose that's why they never learn."

The "they" were, Rose knew, the superior officers in the Police Department, City of New York. The ones who kept giving him jobs for which he was unfit. She put her glass down on the table and reached across and put her hand on the back of his. She left it there only for a moment and picked up her glass again. "Why whisky tonight, Nathan? Instead of the wine?"

"Reaction, I suppose," he said. "I've been—oh, I feel I've been preached at all day. I haven't been but—oh, it was in the air. Tony Cook lighted a cigarette while he was asking one of them some questions and got a tirade. Also, wine is a mocker, strong drink is raging."

"Ours, actually," Rose said. "From Proverbs. But theirs too, of course. Is the Scotch raging, Nathan?"

"Only a little bitter," Nathan said. "It's only that—well, that they take it so hard. Belief ought to be—oh, a tranquil thing. Something accepted. Or, of course, not accepted. Not something to rant about."

She shook her head.

"There are ranters in all religions," she said. "In our own. Jews picket the Israeli mission to the United Nations because autopsies are permitted in Tel Aviv. Arabs declare a holy war against us. Buddhists set themselves on fire. People aren't rational, Nathan. Except—what do the Quakers say?—except me and thee. But that's wrong, I have no doubts about thee. Where was I? I meant to say something."

"That there are ranters in all religious faiths," Nathan said. "That reason is a rarity. That you and I—oh, and others; most people we know, actually—are rational. But we aren't very religious, are we? We belong to a congregation. We observe ancient forms. But with people like these, belief is—oh, a violence. I'm uneasy with violence, Rose."

"And very philosophical this evening," Rose said. "And, you tell me so yourself, very handy with a gun."

He laughed, suddenly. It was a low laugh; almost a contented laugh.

"Violence against the violent," he said. "You let me wander on, dear. I count on that."

"And I on what you call your wandering," Rose said. "Finish your drink, dear, while I get us something to eat. Out of the freezer, I'm afraid, because I was so late." She finished her own drink and stood up. "It will be something kosher." she said, and, gently, laughed down at him.

He smiled up at her and nodded his head. Then he reached a hand out and took her nearest hand and held it for a moment.

He looked with some surprise at his still almost-full glass. He lifted it and tasted again. Not as good as the sweet wine he usually drank. Sharp. Almost harsh. Conceivably, he was carrying reaction to sumptuary laws to an extreme. He sipped again.

On the other hand, the results were pleasant and his stomach did not seem unduly resentful.

It was a little after seven and they had almost finished dinner, which was as kosher as it needed to be—and before which each had had two relaxing, and therefore sinful, drinks—when the telephone rang.

They were finishing coffee at a little after eight, which was early, but Rachel still was holding out for the movie at the Eighth Street Playhouse. They were in a booth in the café section of Charles Restaurant, and curtains were draped down on either side of them which looked as if they might be drawn for seclusion but in fact could not be. On the wall above them was an extremely opulent nude within a heavy gold frame. On the wall above the booth opposite them, which could seat eight and at the moment was doing it, there was another nude, reclining, with a man in the evening dress of the eighteenth century sitting stiffly beside her and looking fixedly in the wrong direction.

Tony Cook was lighting Rachel's cigarette and leaning across the table to do it—and thinking that going to a movie was a hell of a way to waste an evening—when Monsieur Michel came to the booth and stood in view. Monsieur Michel had been "Mike" before Charles reverted to La Belle Epoque. Tony said, "Yes, Mike?"

"Sorry," Mike said, and sounded it—"sorry, but there's a telephone call for you, Mr. Cook."

Which could mean only one thing, and Tony said, "Damn it to hell," and began to edge out of the booth. Rachel, who also knew what it meant, said, "Damn it for me, too," and began to pull up to her shoulders the wrap she was sitting on. She was wearing a black dress which clung to her and moved with her movements. Most becomingly. Tony looked down at her for a second and shook his head and sighed and followed Monsieur Michel toward the telephone.

He was not gone long. When he came back Rachel, with her coat on, was standing outside the booth, and a waiter was beside her, adding up the bill. He put the bill down on the table and Tony put money on it, and they walked out of the café section and past the bar and into Sixth Avenue.

"I take it," Rachel said, "that the evening's shot, Tony. You don't need to take me home."

She said this because he had waved a taxi down and was leading her toward it. She said, "It's only a few blocks. The taxi will take twice as long as walking."

But she got into the taxi. He told the driver Gay Street, and the driver had never heard of it and it had to be explained, and the driver said, "O.K., mister," in a somewhat surly tone. It wasn't a long haul; not long enough. He probably was missing a chance to get something decent on the meter. Rachel looked at Tony and waited.

"This girl you knew," Tony said. "The one who sang in Prentis's choir. She's dead, Rachel. Anyway, somebody's dead in her apartment. Has been since sometime this morning. Maybe late last night. She was found a couple of hours ago. Somebody finally put things together and passed the word. That was Shapiro who called."

Rachel was silent for a time. The taxi went west through Twelfth Street and down Seventh Avenue and into Fourth Street.

"It's dreadful," Rachel said. "Since I've known you there've been so many dreadful things." She stopped and looked at the back of the taxi driver's head. "I don't mean that the way it sounds. Fine things, too. Lovely things. Only—only the once or twice I met her she seemed so alive. And so young." She stopped again. The taxi turned up Sixth and into Waverly Place, headed west. He stopped at Gay Street. He said, "This all right, mister? It's one-way."

Tony said it was all right and paid and tipped—more than he should have done because taxi drivers don't, for the most part, like short hauls. They walked the half block and around the crook in Gay Street, and he waited while she unlocked the door and opened it. He put both hands on her shoulders and pulled her toward him and kissed her and let her go. He said, "Lock yourself in tight. Put the chain on the door," and she said, "Yes, Tony," and then, "Good night, darling." But her voice was dimmed.

He went back to Waverly Place and went left, right and left across Sixth Avenue to a three-story brick house on Washington Place with a cruise car parked in front of it and a uniformed man standing at the top of the sandstone steps. The double inner doors of the entry hall stood open because something had been carried out that way. Tony climbed two flights of carpeted stairs. A door on the third floor was open and he went into a long living room with tall windows at the end of it. One of the two detectives in the room was Charles Pieronelli, who was supposed to be off duty. But Tony himself was supposed to be off duty.

"So," Pieronelli said, "you guys think there's a tie-in."

"Somebody did," Tony said. "She worked for Prentis. Oh, sang in the choir."

"Yeah," Pieronelli said. "We come up with that. Name of Janet Rushton. Pretty little thing, they say. They've taken it away. Matter of fact, they're about finished in there."

He gestured toward a narrow hallway which ran from the living room toward the street side of the apartment.

"Bedroom," Pieronelli said. "Used a pillow, way it looks."

Tony said, "Smothered?" and Pieronelli said "Yeah."

"They're not pretty any more when they've been smothered," Tony said.

"No," Pieronelli said. "Pictures. Publicity shots from her agent, way it looks. She was pretty in the pictures. She—"

A man with a camera came through the narrow hallway, and two men, one of them carrying a flat case, came after him. The police photographer said, "All yours, Charlie," and Charlie Pieronelli said "O.K.," and the three went out of the apartment and clumped down the stairs, their feet heavy on the carpet. Pieronelli opened a door on the left, and they went into the bedroom of the apartment. It was almost as large as the living room and, like the living room, had a fireplace. This fireplace, however, had been walled up.

The bed in the room was a very wide one. Bedclothes had been stripped back on it and there was no pillow. "Took the pillow along, the lab boys did," Pieronelli said. "Lipstick on it. Smeared around."

Tony Cook looked at the bed on which a pretty young

woman had been pinned down and smothered with a pillow. It didn't tell him anything.

"She'd been dead maybe eighteen hours, according to the M.E.'s man," Pieronelli said. "Rigor. She had all her clothes on. Funny thing, according to the guy who found her, her dress had been pulled down to cover her legs. All very neat. Very decent."

"The guy who found her?"

"Name of Minor," Pieronelli said. "Arthur Minor. Says he had a date with her. Going to take her to dinner. We asked him to stay around. He's in the little room we came past. Four rooms in the place. Two big ones and two little ones. One of the little rooms's the kitchen. Off the living room. The other's a sort of guest room, apparently. That's where we're holding—that's where we asked this Minor guy to wait. Want to get his story, Tony?"

"May as well, I guess," Tony said. "The lieutenant's on his way over, but he lives in Brooklyn. Take him a while. I was handy, sort of. Not in here, I think. Back in the living room."

He and Pieronelli went back down the hallway, past a door. "Bathroom," Pieronelli said. "All done in green tile. Quite a place Miss Rushton had here. Must have set her back."

The living room was also quite a place, looked at a second time. The fireplace, with logs piled in it, was of white marble; the long windows had green curtains to the floor. The room was carpeted in a darker green; there were two sofas, both covered in warm yellow, and a deep chair, in the color of the curtains, with a low table beside it. The table had a mirror top. She'd gone to a good deal of trouble to make the room attractive, Tony thought. She had also had to spend a good deal on the room.

She had planned to keep it safe. There was a heavy lock that looked new on the door leading to the outer hall. There was also a guard chain. It was not engaged.

"Snap lock," Pieronelli said. "The super had a key. Not the super, I guess. Seems he owns the building. She didn't have the chain on. Probably let in whoever it was that—"

He stopped because a tall young man had come down the hallway into the room. He had thick brown hair which he had let grow a little long. There was a wave in the brown hair. He had a thin face and, Tony thought, a rather full mouth. The pretty-boy type, Tony thought him, and thought that he was probably in his mid-twenties. And that, from the redness of his eyes, he had been crying.

"Mr. Minor," Pieronelli said. "Mr. Arthur Minor. This is Detective Cook, Mr. Minor. From the homicide squad."

"I've told you all I know about it," Minor said. He had a deep voice; to Tony an unexpectedly deep voice. It wasn't at all what he thought of as a pretty-boy voice.

"We have to go over things a lot," Tony said. "Be sure we get them straight. Way I get it, you came to take Miss Rushton to dinner. Had a date with her?"

"Of course. We—we—were—"

He shook his head and then put both hands up to his forehead, so that the heels of his hands covered his eyes.

"All right," Tony said. "Just take it easy, Mr. Minor. Sit down, why don't you? And just tell us what happened."

Minor sat down. He took his hands down from his head. He said, "Sorry. It's been a hell of a shock. I was fond of Jan."

Tony said, "Sure. Damn bad thing. Just tell us what happened."

What had happened, Arthur Minor told them, was that he had come around at six-thirty to take Janet Rushton out to dinner. Six-thirty had been the time agreed on. Oh, if it mattered, they'd had the date for about ten days. He had pushed the doorbell and waited and nothing had happened. He had tried again, and she had not spoken to him through the intercom and had not pressed the button upstairs which would have released the lock on the inner door. After waiting for a minute or so, he had again pushed on the bell button and again nothing had come of it.

"She was always on the dot," Minor said. "Not like a lot of them. Ever since I've known her she was ready on the dot."

How long had he known her?

"About a year. Dated her a few times. Took her to dinner where we could dance. And—oh, to movies and a couple of times to shows. That sort of thing."

That was all? Not that it mattered too much, but that was all?

"Yes," Minor said. "We were just friends, if that's what you're getting at. We weren't sleeping together. Now and then I'd get the idea of taking her somewhere and calling her up and if she didn't have another date she'd mostly say all right. Last month or so she seemed to have a lot of dates. So I'd call up another girl."

"You said you were fond of her," Tony said.

"Yeah. Only just that. I wasn't tied up with her. Not the way I guess you mean."

"O.K.," Tony said. "You rang her doorbell and she didn't answer it. Then?"

"I waited around maybe five minutes and tried again," Minor said. "Not much point to it, but we did have a date. And she kept dates. So I thought, maybe she's had to go some place—drugstore or some place like that. Or maybe the liquor store. So I went out and walked around a couple of blocks and came back and tried again. On account of she'd never stood me up before, if you know what I mean?"

Tony knew what he meant.

When Minor had returned, which was perhaps in ten minutes or so—it was getting on for seven—he had pressed the bell again, and again nothing had happened.

He had looked in her mailbox, then. Its cover had a grating and he could see into it, and there was mail in it. From the looks, quite a lot of mail. He could see the corner of one of the envelopes, and it had her agent's return address on it.

"The guy who handled her," Minor said. "She's—" He paused and his thin face grew longer. "She was a singer," he said, and there was a shake in his deep voice. "Cafés, mostly. Places like that. She was in a musical last winter. Had a good number. But it folded. She'd had a job singing in some sort of choir the last few weeks. Just to fill in."

"Yes," Tony said. "An evangelist's choir. The Reverend Mr. Prentis's choir."

Minor merely shook his head. The name seemed to mean nothing to him. Apparently he didn't read newspapers or look at TV news.

"You looked in her mailbox," Tony said. "Saw there was mail still in it. So?"

"Way it is," Minor said. "You go down and look in the mailbox the first thing. First thing in the morning. See if your agent's come through with anything. Do it myself."

"You're in the theater too, Mr. Minor?"

"Hell, no. I write stories. Pieces, if you know what I mean. Had one in *Esquire* last month. Got some out with my agent now. So first thing in the morning, you look in the mailbox. And if she hadn't this morning, she must be out of town or something. Only we had a date and if she'd got an out-of-town job she'd have given me a ring. So—so I got to thinking maybe something had happened."

Tony Cook nodded his head.

"I knew—anyway, I'd met—the man who owns this building. Lives in the basement apartment, only they call it the garden apartment, and the floor above. He and his wife and a couple of kids. Anyway, I've seen kids in the garden from—from this room. Name of Brady. Something like that. He's a lawyer or something. So, when I started to get worried about Jan, I rang his bell."

Brady had, after a minute or two, come along the first-floor hall and looked out into the entryway. He had recognized Minor. "He's got a memory for faces, I guess," Minor said. "Only met him once. Jan and I were going out and he came up through the basement gate and Jan introduced us."

Brady had let Minor in and had listened to him—listened and looked doubtful. Perhaps Miss Rushton had merely confused her dates. People did sometimes. He didn't want to disturb a tenant. Especially a good tenant like Miss Rushton. Quiet girl. Didn't throw any wild parties or that sort of thing. Reliable sort of young woman.

"I told him that that was just the point," Minor told Tony Cook and Charles Pieronelli. "Told him she wasn't the kind of girl who'd get confused about her dates. So maybe something had happened to her. Maybe she'd got sick or something. Finally he said, all right, we could go up and knock on her door."

They had climbed the stairs and knocked on the door and she had not come to the door. Minor had called through the door. Finally he had turned to Brady and said, "You've got a key to her apartment, haven't you?"

"Sure," Brady said. "It's my house. Only, it's her apartment. I've got no right to—"

But, finally he had gone back downstairs for his passkey. He had put the key in the lock and said, "Won't do any good if she's got the chain up, you know," and turned the key.

The chain had not been up. Brady had opened the door a few inches and called, "Miss Rushton?" and, when there was no answer, called again, more loudly. Then he had said, "Guess she's not here," and started to close the door again.

"I said we might as well be sure, now we'd gone that far," Minor said. "And he said, 'It's trespass, you know,' but didn't try to stop me. And—well, her bedroom door wasn't closed and I looked in and—and there she was. I called her again and then yelled to Brady and—well, he came on in, finally."

He stopped for a moment and, again, ground the heels of his hands against his forehead. Without taking them down, he said, "She looked as if she'd just—just lain down with her clothes on and—and gone to sleep. Only, the pillow was over her face and—sort of pressed down. You could still see where somebody had pressed on it. And I went over and touched her and—she was cold." He paused. "Dead cold," he said. "I tried to lift her up and—well, I knew then."

"Rigor had begun to pass off when the ambulance man got here," Pieronelli said. "It was warm in the room. Makes a difference sometimes."

"Yes, Charlie," Tony Cook said. "I've read the books. When you first saw her, Mr. Minor. You thought she was just asleep? Had lain down to rest with her clothes on and fallen asleep?"

"That's the way it looked. At first."

"Not as if she'd struggled? I mean, tossed about?"

"Just stretched out. On her back. Her—her dress all smoothed out. As if—oh, as if she'd been careful not to rumple it or anything. She was wearing a—I don't know what you'd call it. A dress-up dress or something. Silk or something like it. A pale green dress. She—she liked things green."

"As if she were dressed to go out?"

"Yes. But—but not for our date. I knew that when I tried to lift her up."

"Like I said," Pieronelli said, "she'd been dead maybe eighteen hours, according to the doc."

"Yes," Cook said. "Mr. Minor, you said that for the last month or so Miss Rushton had been tied up pretty much of the time. When you tried to make dates with her."

"Yeah."

"Made you think that, perhaps, she'd—oh, hit it off with someone else? Was seeing someone often?"

Minor shrugged his shoulders. He said, "Look, I told you the way it was. Now and then I'd call her up and ask her to go to dinner or something. Sometimes she'd be free and sometimes she wouldn't. So I supposed she had dates with other guys, and that was O.K. too. Girls like her—well, a lot of guys want to take them out. I—I didn't have any option on her."

"But would have liked to have had, maybe?"

"I told you I was fond of her. All right, maybe I'd been getting fonder of her the more I knew her. She—she was a hell of a sweet kid."

"Upset this last month or so, when she was tied up so much?"

"Not to say upset. Disappointed, you could call it. Not pining away, if that's what you're getting at. And, not jealous, mister. And last night, before you ask me, I was at a party over on Twelfth Street. A biggish sort of party with a lot of people I know. From around eight-thirty until God knows when. Three in the morning, maybe."

He gave the address of the party and the name of his hosts.

"I hadn't been planning to ask you," Cook said. "But since you've brought it up, Mr. Minor. At the party until about three this morning. Then?"

"I took a girl home," Minor said. "She lives uptown on the east side. Girl I've known for years. And—all right, I stayed around a while. Then I went home and went to bed. All right?"

"Perfectly all right," Cook said and raised his eyebrows at Pieronelli.

"Yes," Pieronelli said. "We know where Mr. Minor lives. A few blocks from here."

"You've had a bad experience, Mr. Minor," Tony Cook said. "Probably like to go get yourself a drink. Dinner maybe."

"Jesus Christ," Minor said, "you think I'm hungry?"

"No," Tony Cook said. "I don't suppose you are. Go do what you want to do. If we need to, we'll get in touch with you."

Minor went back along the hallway and returned with a topcoat over his arm. He went out through the living-room door.

"Only door to the apartment?" Cook asked Pieronelli, and Pieronelli shook his head. He said, "Kitchen door. Locked and chained."

"You've talked to this man Brady? The one who owns the house?"

"Clifford Brady," Pieronelli said. "Yeah, Tony. Tells it the same way. Says Minor acted just like you'd expect a man to act who'd found a girl friend stretched out dead. He—"

The door from the outer hall opened, and Lieutenant Nathan Shapiro came into the room. He looked tired.

8

There were half a dozen glossy photographic prints in a desk in Janet Rushton's bedroom. Pieronelli brought them out to the living room and gave them to Shapiro. They were all of a blonde young woman with the brightness and the contours of youth in her face—a pretty girl, but like many pretty girls. Underlines were pasted to the bottoms of the prints—"Janet Rushton, Soprano"—and a list of places where she had sung. Most of the places were in New York. One of them was in Las Vegas. Some of the photographs were in soft focus, and in those Janet looked a little wistful. On the backs of the photographs had been stamped "Talent, Inc.," with an address in the Forties.

Shapiro selected two from the half dozen—two in which the focus was the hardest. He gave one to Pieronelli and said, "Want to get us some copies made?" and Pieronelli said, "Sure, Lieutenant. He went back into the bedroom and returned with two envelopes the prints would fit in and said, "What you want, Lieutenant? And we've got her address book."

Shapiro nodded his head sadly. He put the print he had kept in one of the envelopes and said, "We may as well both go, Tony," and led the way out of the apartment.

One thing about him, Tony Cook thought, he never throws his weight around. He doesn't tell Charlie Pieronelli what to do because he knows Charlie already knows what to do, and what to start others doing.

The wind hurried through Washington Place and blew them east. It was a cold wind. It had cleared the air; when you looked up you could see half a moon and clouds hurrying across it. The cold wind blew them diagonally across Washington Square Park and held them back a little—tried to make them tilt a little—up Fifth to Eighth Street. It blew them east through Eighth Street to the Village Brawl, and by that time Shapiro knew what there was to know about the finding of Janet Rushton's body, snatching Tony Cook's words as the wind blew them past him.

"Probably just the way he says it was," Shapiro said, as they went down the steps to the doors with pictures of naked girls pasted on them.

It would not, of course, be left at "probably." Things would be checked out; the party Arthur Minor said he had been to would be checked out; the girl he had taken home would be found and asked about being taken home. They would find out more about Arthur Minor and more about Janet Rushton. There would be dozens of men working on it, directly. And all over the city, policemen were asking clerks in hardware stores about recent purchases of entirely ordinary ice picks. Of this last, it was a thousand to one nothing would come. Which is no reason for not spreading out a net.

A doorman in uniform said "Good evening, gentlemen." He led them to and opened the door of the Village Brawl. It was a little after nine, and the combo was making loud noises on its platform—sax and guitar and piano and a trumpet. The trumpet was pretty good, Tony thought. Nathan prefers Brahms.

The restaurant was only moderately filled. A man in a dinner jacket came up to them and said, "Two?" and then, "Oh." His voice went down on the "Oh."

"Yes," Shapiro said. "Back again, Mr. Granzo. Mr. Schmidt around?"

Granzo repeated the name as if he had never heard it before. "Yes," Shapiro said. "The waiter." Granzo said, "Oh, Emile," and looked back into the restaurant. "Don't see—yeah, there he comes." He did not point; he indicated with a movement of his head.

The man he indicated was tall and blond and looked young. He was carrying a small tray with glasses on it above his head and circling the dance floor on which three couples were dancing. He carried his tray to a table halfway down the room and served the drinks from it. Then he turned and started back toward the entrance of the bar.

"Pretty busy just now," Granzo said. "Band's just started up and they're beginning to come in. Maybe if you don't—"

He stopped because Shapiro was not paying attention to him. Shapiro was moving between tables in the direction Emile Schmidt had taken, and Tony Cook was moving after him. Granzo shrugged his shoulders. He said, "Two, m'sieu?" to a heavy-set man behind a girl who might have been his daughter and probably wasn't, which was none of Granzo's business. He said, "This way, sir," and led the way.

There were stools part of the way along the length of the bar, and a man and a girl were sitting on two of them. At the far end there was a sign which said, "Service Only," and there Emile Schmidt was putting a tray on the bar and leaning toward the bartender. Emile wore a maroon jacket with dark green lapels and so did the bartender. There was a second bartender, in the same uniform. He was polishing glasses.

He put a glass down on the bar when Shapiro and Cook went in and moved up to the bar and looked expectant. Shapiro shook his head, and he and Cook went to the far end, where the bartender was putting cocktail glasses with crushed ice in them on Emile Schmidt's tray. It looked like being a good bar, Tony thought. Maybe some day he and Rachel might try it. She was one hell of a good dancer.

Shapiro said, "Mr. Schmidt?" to Schmidt and Schmidt said, "M'sieu?" Shapiro would rather have expected "Bitte?"

"Police," Shapiro said.

It did not disturb Emile Schmidt, but this time he said "Yeah?" instead of "M'sieu?"

Shapiro took the glossy print out of its envelope and held it out to Emile Schmidt and said, "Ever see her before?"

Schmidt took the photograph and moved so that the light fell on it. He looked at it carefully. He said, "A looker, ain't she?"

"Yes," Shapiro said. "Remember ever seeing her before?"

"Somebody I ought to know?" Schmidt said, and looked at the picture again.

"I don't know," Shapiro said. "Possibly."

"Can't say I—" Schmidt said and stopped with that and

looked at the picture again. Then he said, "Seems like maybe I—" and stopped again and looked at the photograph again. Then he said, "Customer, maybe?"

You don't lead witnesses. A led witness is no good to anybody. Shapiro said, "Could be, Mr. Schmidt."

"Lot of them look like that," Schmidt said.

Cagy? Nathan wondered. Or just not wanting to stick his neck out? Or, as was most likely, only not sure. A waiter sees a lot of people. He doesn't often look at them closely, even when they are pretty girls. Well, it had always been an outside—

"*Wait* a min-ute," Schmidt said. "Last night? With this—with this guy got killed?"

"Up to you," Shapiro said. "Just take your time, Mr. Schmidt."

Schmidt moved off a little, where the light was better. The bartender took two small decanters out of a bed of crushed ice and put them on the tray and poured into them from a shaker. He put a dish of slivers of lemon peel on the tray. One hell of a good bar, Tony thought. They go to trouble even when nobody's watching them.

"I tell you," Schmidt said, turning back. "It could be. I don't say for sure it is, but it could be. I was hopping and I just put these two drinks down, but it could be this is the girl. Matter of fact, I sort of think it is. Not that I could swear to it. Come down to that, I couldn't, mister. But it sure as hell looks like her."

It wasn't much and it wasn't good. But, Nathan Shapiro thought, it was what they were going to get. For now, anyway. Shapiro held a hand out, and Schmidt gave him back the photograph of a pretty girl who was now lying in the Bellevue morgue, unless they had already gone to work on her. Shapiro and Tony Cook went back into the main restaurant. It had filled up a good deal in the few minutes they had been out of it. They had to wait near the entrance for Granzo to come back from seating people. The music, to Shapiro, seemed even louder than before.

It was André Brideaux's night off. A detective's life is full of minor tribulations. The hat-check girl, shown the picture, said, "Mister, I see hundreds like her."

"She probably would have come in alone last night," Shapiro said. "Meeting somebody here. Would have had some sort of wrap to check."

"Nope," the hat check girl said. "You don't want me to lie to you, do you, mister?"

There was a cab in front of the Village Brawl, and a man was leaning into it paying the driver. The light went on on top of the cab and Tony said, "Hold it!" and reached for the door handle. The driver said, "Look, mister, I'm due in. Which way you want to go?"

"Uptown," Tony said, and got into the cab and Shapiro got in after him.

"Listen," the driver said, "the garage is over in—"

Shapiro gave him the address in West Twentieth Street. The driver turned around and looked at him. He said, "That's a police station, ain't it?"

"Yes," Shapiro said, "that's a police station, Mr. Brekowitch."

The names and photographs are on visible cards in all New York taxicabs. Shapiro looks at them. Like all policemen, he wishes more taxi riders did.

The driver slapped his flag down. Traffic wasn't bad to West Twentieth Street. It was too late for the theater crowd. Big trucks dozed at curbs. Shapiro paid the hacker, and the "Off Duty" sign went up on top of the cab. The driver had really meant it. It wasn't the usual time for a change in shifts. That comes most often late in the afternoon, just when people finish shopping or leave offices and try to get home. But taxi drivers are unpredictable.

Cook and Shapiro climbed to the squad room of Homicide South. They went into Shapiro's small office and turned on the lights. Shapiro's In basket was full, ready for morning. He sat at the desk and shuffled papers and rubbed his eyes, because typed reports tended to blur. It had been a long day—a long day with nothing accomplished. "Count that day lost—" and what was the rest of it?

Tony Cook sat across the desk and waited.

Detectives of the downtown precinct would be calling numbers listed in Janet Rushton's address book. They would be ringing doorbells at addresses listed in it. Some of the people listed would be home, but most would not. The names she had written down would, probably, be of friends of her own age. Most of them would not be sitting home at nine-thirty in the evening.

Detectives would have quit asking in hardware stores about an ordinary ice pick, because hardware stores would be closed. They would still be showing a photograph of Ralph Farmington to bartenders in the area around the Hotel Wexley, because the bars would be open.

"She was slugged first," Shapiro said, and slid a copy of the preliminary report from the Bellevue morgue across the desk to Tony Cook.

The subject had been five feet four inches tall and had weighed a hundred and three pounds. She had died of asphyxiation. Before death she had been hit heavily on the left side of the jaw, probably with a fist. It was probable that the blow had rendered her unconscious. She had been in her early twenties.

"Expecting somebody, probably," Shapiro said. "Didn't call down to ask who it was. May have left the door unlocked. If she didn't want bells ringing and the latch clattering. Obviously didn't fasten the chain."

"Yeah," Tony said. "And opened the door and whoever it was slugged her. They ask for it, don't they?"

They asked for it.

"If she was the girl with Prentis," Tony said, "figure Prentis was the man she was expecting? Had left the door unlocked for? Why would he have let her go on ahead? It could be risky for a girl by herself at two in the morning, or whenever it was."

"I don't know. Didn't want to be seen with her, maybe."

"Or maybe he was already dead."

"Yes. Maybe he was already dead. And she cut and ran."

"Only," Tony said, "Rachel says she seemed like a nice kid. Not the sort of thing a nice kid would do, you'd think."

Shapiro said "Mmmm." You can't tell what a nice girl may do. You can guess, but you can't be sure. At the moment, Nathan Shapiro couldn't tell what anybody would do. About these people he couldn't even guess. He went back to sorting reports.

Henry Pruitt, treasurer of the Mission of Redemption, Inc., had taken a plane out of St. Louis for New York. He might be in New York by now. Or he might be locked in a cylinder with eighty others—a hundred others—going round and round above New York, waiting for a cleared runway. Coming east to preside over the dissolution of the Mission of Redemption, Inc. Which was what it would come to, presumably, with the Voice silenced. And—

Shapiro said, "Mmmm," with an inflection and slid another sheet of paper across the desk to Tony Cook. This one was a report from the police of Little Rock, Arkansas. Mrs. Jonathan Prentis's name appeared on a list of passengers in an airplane out of Little Rock for St. Louis on Sunday, February 22. Tony said, "Uh?"

"She thinks it's sinful to travel on Sunday," Shapiro said. "She was supposed to have come east with the main group, which got here on March second. She allowed herself a lot of time in Saint Louis."

"Could be," Tony said, "she likes Saint Louis better than Little Rock. Or, could be she didn't stay in Saint Louis. Could be she came on here. On her own."

"Yes," Shapiro said. "She was asleep at eleven o'clock last night, according to Mrs. Mathews. But—she might have waked up. We'll have to ask her."

"Came east," Tony said. "Scouted around. Found out her husband was going in for fun and games. Did see him going out of his room last night. Wearing civvies. Put two and two together and—came up with an ice pick?"

"We'll have to ask," Shapiro said. "See if they've got a car for us, Tony."

Tony Cook used the telephone. Nathan Shapiro shuffled papers together and put a paperweight on top of them. They went uptown in a police car, Shapiro carrying the glossy photograph of Janet Rushton in its manila envelope. They did not call up on the house phone in the Hotel Wexley. They went up to the sixth floor in one of the elevators. Tony started down the corridor toward the rooms at the end of it—the rooms across the hall from each other. But Nathan said, "Not yet,

Tony," and went across the hall and rang a doorbell. He had to ring it several times before the door opened.

Ralph Farmington was fully dressed in a dark suit and a white shirt. After he had opened the door he pulled the knot of his necktie tighter. He said, "Oh, you again. The Reverend isn't here. Gone out to Kennedy to meet Pruitt. And I—I was just going downstairs for a cup of coffee."

He stepped out of the way to let Shapiro and Cook go into the living room of the suite. He watched Shapiro go across the room and sit behind the desk.

"You act like something new's come up," Farmington told Shapiro.

"Yes," Shapiro said. "Something new's come up, Mr. Farmington. Come over and have a look at this, will you?"

He took the photograph of a dead girl out of its envelope and laid it on the desk, and Farmington crossed the room and picked it up. Tony stood near the door, his back to the wall. He leaned against the wall.

Farmington looked at the photograph. He read the underlines taped to it. He turned it over and looked at the back with "Talent, Inc." stamped on it. He said, "Yeah. One of the girls. Something special about her?"

"For us, yes," Shapiro said. "She's dead, Mr. Farmington. Killed some time last night. In her apartment. Probably after the Reverend Prentis was killed."

Farmington went over and sat on a sofa and looked at Nathan Shapiro for some seconds. Then, to Shapiro's surprise, he said, "Jesus Christ." He did not say it in a tone of prayer.

"Also," Shapiro said, "she may have been with Mr. Prentis at this restaurant. Where he was killed. You got any idea how that could have come about, Mr. Farmington?"

Farmington shook his head—his rather handsome head, with gray just beginning to show in his yellow hair. He said, "Why should I, Lieutenant?"

"She was one of the singers you recruited," Shapiro said. "Interviewed, I suppose. Auditioned?"

"No," Farmington said. "Look, I had a hundred and eighty to round up. More, for spares. Joe Westclock says she's O.K., so I say send her around. Knew Joe wouldn't let me down."

"Westclock?"

"Runs the agency. Used to handle me in the old days. This kid wasn't going to sing a solo or anything."

"You engaged several of your singers through Mr. Westclock? Just—just what, Mr. Farmington? So many sopranos? So many contraltos?"

"And tenors and baritones," Farmington said. "Sure, that was pretty much the way. Joe came through with maybe twenty. Maybe thirty. It's all down somewhere. There are a lot of singers kicking around loose in New York. And a lot of flesh peddlers handling them."

"You didn't interview them personally?"

"Had them show up at the rehearsal hall Ted Acton got us. Sorted them out and gave them the music and went at it. With the regulars helping, of course. The ones who travel with us. Takes a week, ten days, to get them shaped up."

"No special attention to individuals?"

"Not unless they sing off-key. Doesn't happen very often. They're mostly pros. Not big-time pros, but they can carry tunes. Damn near anybody can sing hymns, Lieutenant."

Nathan said he saw. He said that Mr. Farmington made it very clear. He said, "So Miss Rushton didn't stand out in any way? As an individual?"

"No. Just one of the crowd."

"But," Nathan said, "you recognized her quickly enough from her picture, Mr. Farmington. She was a good-looking girl. One any man might notice, I'd think."

"Look," Farmington said, "I told you before, or near enough. I don't look. I listen. I'm not hiring a chorus line."

You are going out of character, Shapiro thought. First time around you were one of the godly. When you remembered, anyway. Now you're—I guess it's theater. A producer, who knows his way around. What Shapiro said was, "I see, Mr. Farmington." But then he said, "I suppose you did look at pictures, Mr. Farmington? Of singers Mr. Westclock thought he could get for you?"

"Joe and a dozen other agents. Sometimes. They've all got pictures of their clients. Most jobs, it makes a difference what the boys and girls look like. More than what they sound like, most of the time."

"The ones you hired through Mr. Westclock? Miss Rushton and the others?"

"I guess so. Sure, I remember. Joe wanted me to look at them. Joe and I're sort of old friends. Sort of friends, anyway."

"Other good-looking young women?"

"A couple of others. Blondes. Like he—"

He stopped speaking. He stopped abruptly.

Shapiro waited for some seconds without saying anything, but looking at the big, good-looking man on the sofa. Then he said, "Yes, Mr. Farmington? You were going to say?"

"Nothing."

Shapiro shook his head, sadly. He said, "No. That's not good enough, is it?" His voice was very sad and very tired. "Not nearly good enough, is it? You—what, Mr. Farmington? Showed these pictures of pretty blondes to Mr. Prentis? For him to pick from?"

"Hell," Farmington said. "It wasn't the way you make it sound. He—all right. This week or so the Voice spent sort of preparing himself. Getting to know about the city he was going —going to redeem. See what I mean?"

"No," Shapiro said, "I can't say I do. But go on."

"Thing is," Farmington said, and now he spoke slowly, and, Shapiro thought, not with confidence. Now he spoke like a man feeling his way with care. "Thing is, you come into a city cold, the way he had to. Helps if you have somebody who can —oh, show you around. Go places with you where a man by himself would—sort of stand out. Particularly a man who wouldn't look as if he belonged in places the Reverend Prentis wanted to find out about. See what I mean now, Lieutenant?"

"Yes," Shapiro said. "A guide. And—a cover, Mr. Farmington?"

He could call it that.

"A pretty young girl. Preferably a blonde. He usually wanted a blonde—guide?"

"Yes. After all, he married a blonde. Ten years ago. Hope must have been a looker. All right now, come to that. Only—"

He stopped again. After some seconds, Shapiro repeated the word "only?"

"Look," Farmington said, "I don't know anything about it. Not to say know. Only thing is—well, I'd figure her a cold fish, sort of. Way you get feelings about people. Maybe they're no good—the feelings, I mean. Maybe Hope's a hot number for all I know."

"Sure," Shapiro said. "Sometimes it's hard to tell. You gave Mr. Prentis a—call it a selection. Pictures of a few girls. With their addresses?"

"I guess so."

"And Miss Rushton was one of them?"

"Yes. Way I remember it."

"She lived down in the Village, Mr. Farmington. Quite near the hotel where Mr. Prentis was staying."

"Did she? I wouldn't know."

"Quite near," Shapiro said. "The—the mission has been in New York before. Several times over a period of years, I gather. During these periods of preparation, did Mr. Prentis usually stay downtown? In Greenwich Village?"

"I wouldn't know. Anyway, I don't remember. Hell, I wasn't his keeper, Lieutenant."

Shapiro said, "No, of course not," and did not add what, he suspected, Ralph Farmington might have been to the Reverend Jonathan Prentis. Shapiro stood up from behind the desk and looked across the room at Tony Cook and then, because of what was in Tony's face, said, "Yes, Detective Cook?"

"Nothing important," Cook said. "I just wondered what these singers got paid. For their choir singing."

He looked at Farmington, still sitting on the sofa.

"No secret about it," Farmington said. "It's down on the books. Fifty dollars for each appearance. They've got to make their living."

"Sure," Tony said. "They were paid through their agents, I suppose? And their agents took their cuts?"

"Sure," Farmington said. "Nobody's in business for the fun of it."

"No," Tony said. "Ten per cent, I suppose?"

Farmington supposed so. That was standard.

"Happen to have a list of these singers?" Tony asked him. "Names and addresses?"

"Mrs. Mathews," Farmington said. "She sends out the checks. She and her girls. What the hell for, Detective Cook?"

It was Shapiro who answered. He said, "Probably for nothing, Mr. Farmington. We get a lot of odds and ends together, and mostly nothing comes of it. But—Mrs. Mathews will have the list? With home addresses?"

"Yeah," Farmington said. "Checks go to the agents, of course. But we have the addresses."

Shapiro raised his eyebrows at Tony Cook and Cook shook his head. "All right, Mr. Farmington," Shapiro said. "You've been helpful. Go and get your coffee."

It wasn't an order, but Farmington acted as if it were. He went out of the room abruptly, with a kind of eagerness.

"What it comes to," Tony said, "he was pimping for the Reverend. To put an ugly word to it."

"We don't know," Shapiro said. "Perhaps just running a guide service."

Tony used one word to answer that.

"Yes," Nathan Shapiro said. "You're probably right. And, you think kickbacks from the boys and girls, don't you?"

"A chance of it," Cook said. "He's—well, he could be the type, Nate."

"Yes," Nathan said. "He could be. Not as religious as he sounded at first. We'll have to ask around, Tony."

9

Nathan Shapiro stood on a windy subway platform and waited for an express to Brooklyn and shivered. Rose had been right, of course. All winter she had been right in urging him to get a new and heavier overcoat. But by the time he had been ready to say, "All right, Rose," it had been March, and in March spring may be supposed to be just around the corner. This year it had, obviously, missed the turn.

Trains run less frequently as evening turns to night; by ten-thirty it is a long time between trains—a long, cold time and a dreary one. It was dreary especially for a man who had been up since five and had spent a day getting nowhere. He and Tony Cook had got nowhere—nowhere to speak of, anyway—from the time Ralph Farmington had gone to get coffee—or whatever he had gone to get—and the time Shapiro had said, "Let's call it a day, Tony. There'll always be a tomorrow." Not that there was any special reason to look forward to tomorrow.

They had found Theodore Acton, who arranged transportation for the mission. They had found him a wiry and indignant man who did not use Biblical terms and wanted to know when he could get his people out of here, because a floor of a hotel costs money and it takes time to charter an airplane. And, if Shapiro did not realize it, money was going to stop coming in with the Voice no longer to be heard. Shapiro had hoped it wouldn't be too long. Had Acton arranged air transportation for Mrs. Jonathan Prentis from Little Rock, Arkansas, to Saint Louis, Missouri, on Sunday, February twenty-second?

Acton had not. Anyway, Mrs. Prentis would not travel on a Sunday. She thought it sinful to travel on a Sunday.

Sinful or not, she had traveled on that Sunday, unless the airline's passenger list was wrong.

Acton knew nothing about it. If she had, she had made her own reservation.

Had she flown to New York on the chartered plane from Saint Louis which reached Kennedy on March second, and had she been met by Acton and taken, with the others, to the Hotel Wexley?

"I told you that," Acton said. "You people don't remember things very well, do you? Sure she did."

The speed of air traffic, when the weather isn't bad, when planes aren't stacked over airports, can complicate matters for a detective. Mrs. Prentis might have flown to St. Louis on February 22 and then on to New York. To check on her husband and his "guide." And then, in hours—or, of course, days—back to St. Louis to board a chartered plane with the others and fly back to New York. Which probably would come to mean a long checking of passenger lists, which would be tedious for the Police Department, City of New York. And people do not need to be truthful about their names.

Shapiro's train clattered to the platform, and Shapiro got on it. One thing about ten-thirty at night was that you could sit down while you went under the East River to Brooklyn. The train was warmer than the platform had been.

Had Mrs. Prentis known about her husband's guided tours in search of the more sinful areas of New York? If she had known, would she have felt strongly enough to do something about them? Like sticking an ice pick in her husband's back?

Shapiro would be able to try to guess about that when he got to see Mrs. Prentis, he thought as the train roared into the tunnel under the river. He had not got to see her that evening, which was one reason he had decided to call it an evening. (Another reason that he was tired, which left his mind even more fuzzy than usual. If, he thought, that's possible.)

They had gone to Mrs. Mathews's room on their way, they had hoped, to Mrs. Prentis's. They had stubbed out cigarettes and knocked on the door and heard, through it, "Go away, whoever you are. I'm busy."

She had been told who they were and she had said, "Not again," but had let them in.

Why did they want a list of the singers Mr. Farmington had engaged?

"Because one of them is dead," Shapiro said, and told her what of that he thought she needed to know. This included the name of Janet Rushton.

"We sent out her check yesterday. No, day before. To her agent. It should have got to her—oh!"

"Yes," Shapiro said. "She won't cash it."

"All right," Mrs. Mathews said, "the Lord giveth and the Lord taketh away. Blessed be the name of the Lord. I can't give you the list unless Mr. Pruitt approves. And he's in Saint Louis."

"No," Shapiro said. "He's on his way here. Mr. Higgs has gone to meet him at the airport. Is there something secret about this list of names, Mrs. Mathews? Because I'm sure you want to help us find out about Mr. Prentis's death."

She said, "I don't see—oh, I guess it'll be all right."

She had gone back to the desk she had got up from to let them in. She opened a drawer of the desk and took out of it sheets clipped together. "Carbons," she said. She handed the clipped sheets to Shapiro. "Grouped by agents," she said.

Shapiro could see they were, and nodded his head. There were several pages of names. Some were followed by street addresses and some were not. The names under the heading "Talent, Inc." had street addresses after them. Shapiro folded the sheets and gave them to Tony Cook, who put them in his pocket.

"Now," Nathan Shapiro said, "We'd like to see Mrs. Prentis. Few questions we want to ask her. About last night."

"No," Mrs. Mathews said. "And this time I mean no. The poor thing's had enough already. Enough to bear, without being badgered."

"We'll try not to—"

"And anyway you can't, because she's under sedation. When she woke up this evening she got hysterical, and no wonder. So the Reverend Higgs said we ought to get a doctor to give her something and we did. And he gave her something so she could rest. And said she wasn't to be disturbed."

"The hotel doctor?"

"Yes. A Dr. Abernathy. And you can ask him if you don't believe me."

"Oh," Nathan said, "we believe you. We'll drop by tomorrow to see Mrs. Prentis."

There hadn't been any reason to check with Dr. Abernathy. There was no reason Mrs. Mathews should lie about it. There is no reason for anybody to tell a lie which can be instantly disproved. Which Mrs. Mathews, who was alert and businesslike under piety, would know perfectly well.

Shapiro did check, by telephone, on the TWA flight out of St. Louis that Henry Pruitt had taken. It had been due at ten. The ETA was now midnight. Weather conditions had been adverse and departure from St. Louis had been delayed.

The metronome which ticks in the minds of commuters and subway riders told Shapiro that the station the train was slowing for was his station. The wind buffeted him the few blocks to his apartment. He stopped at a newsstand and bought a copy of the bulldog edition of the *Daily News*, and the blind man who sold it to him said, "Evening, Lieutenant. It's getting colder."

In the apartment, Rose was sitting on the sofa in front of the fireplace and had turned on the electric fire. She got up when he came in and looked at him carefully and then said, "You look done in, Nathan. Can I get you something?"

"No," he said, "I'm all right," and, looking down at her, putting hands on her shoulders, he all at once felt all right. He took off his jacket, and she took his gun when it was unstrapped, as she did when she thought he was very tired, and put it on its shelf.

The *Daily News* had "Girl Singer Slain" on the second page, and the name was right, or near enough. (The name was "Reshton," but that was near enough.) The story was only three paragraphs long and the *News* did not connect it with the murder of the Reverend Jonathan Prentis. "Police Seek Ice Pick Slayer." (Story on Page 3.) The *News*, for this edition, described Janet Reshton as a nightclub singer.

But the *News* would make the connection. Probably it was made in the edition already slapping out of the presses. It wouldn't be a three-paragraph story by now. And for the *News*, and for the New York *Times* as well, the murder of the Reverend Jonathan Prentis would no longer be a second-day story.

"Police See Link—" Something like that, anyway.

He wished one policeman saw anything clearly, and went to bed.

Rose Shapiro lay very quietly in the bed next her husband's until she heard his breathing grow slow and deep—the breathing of sleep. Then she slept.

A bell clattered, yanking Tony Cook from sleep. He groped for the telephone, which was hiding in this still unfamiliar room. He found it and lifted the receiver, and the bell kept on clattering and he got the dial tone. He put the telephone back in its cradle and groped over it and turned off the alarm clock. It was still dark. Probably it was raining again. Or, from the temperature in the room, snowing. He shivered out of bed and to the window and pulled the Venetian blind up and closed the window. There was sun on the building across the street. It was dark in the apartment because it was a dark apartment. He would have sunshine to walk streets in.

He was on the eight-to-four and he was going to be late checking in. No. That had been set up the night before. He was going from address to address to ring doorbells and ask about kickbacks. It had been his idea, his stab in the dark. So, he was stuck with it. He put coffee on and showered and shaved and put a warm robe on while the turned-up thermostat set the temperature right in the apartment. He made breakfast and ate it and thought about Rachel Farmer, about whom lately he was thinking too damn much.

He had been tempted to call her up when he had got home the night before. Not with any idea that they might pick up the broken pieces of the evening. Just to see that she was all right. There was no reason she shouldn't be all right. She'd been all right for years before he met her. Probably she would be asleep. With nothing else to do, she slept easily, as a cat sleeps. Or perhaps she had gone to the movie they had planned to go to. Or perhaps she had gone somewhere else, with someone else.

That would be up to her. She didn't have to tell him what

she did when they weren't together. It wasn't that way with them. Sure it wasn't. If he called her now and she didn't answer, it would be because she had decided to go on to the movie. Or, of course, somewhere else. Which wasn't any of his business.

He took his hand off the telephone he had been, absently, stroking. He went to bed. After some little time he went to sleep.

He ran hot water over his breakfast dishes and set them in the rack to drain. He finished dressing. He got the lists of names from his jacket pocket and spread them out on a table. There were certainly a hell of a lot of names; it had been a hell of a big choir. It had, on the whole, been a hell of a big operation. And what would happen to it now? Would this Higgs guy, who apparently had backed the Voice up, go in now to pinch-hit? Farmington was sure he wouldn't, because he didn't have the voice for it. Or, Tony thought, what they called the presence for it. But Farmington could be wrong. Farmington didn't seem to be running things. Except the choir, of course. It had sure as hell been a big choir.

Thirty or so names to the page, in double-spaced typing. Six pages. Split them up and get some more men on them? Precinct squad? After all, it was their kill. Both of the kills were theirs.

But it's my notion, Tony thought. My stab in the dark. Take a sampling and if anything comes of that, pass it along. If it's an issue at all, it's probably a side issue. Suppose Farmington had been taking kickbacks from his boys and girls and suppose the Reverend Prentis had found out about it. Reason for murder? Well, you can never tell what may be a reason for murder. Nate thinks there is never a reason for murder. Not a real reason; not a reason that would stand up in a sane mind. All the same, people do kill other people.

Some of the names with home addresses listed; most with only the names of agents for address. Take his sampling from the easiest. Start with those he could group and, preferably, with those who lived within walking distance; lived downtown, as now he lived downtown.

He began to make a list. West Twelfth Street. Charles

Street. Waverly Place. East Eighteenth. Over in the Stuyvesant Square area that would be. Hell, Gay Street. Just around the jog from Rachel's place. Leave that until last. Say about lunch-time. Not that she would be there. A hundred to one against that. She would be at some photographer's studio, posing with clothes on. Or in a painter's studio, probably without clothes on. Drafty places, she said those were. And they'd be drafty today, from the way the wind was rattling his own windows. You'd think a girl would catch cold that way, but she never seemed to. She—

I'm letting this thing get out of hand, Tony told himself. We have fun together. We play games together. That's the way we both want it, and that's all we want of it. Sure it is. Thompson Street. That'll be a ways down below the Square. A dozen within walking distance. Plenty for a sample. Plenty to start with.

He put his jacket on, with his gun under it in accordance with regulations, and made sure his badge was in his pocket. He put a topcoat on and went out and got about it. It was only a little after nine, which probably would be the crack of dawn for most of them.

Stacey Holmes, contralto; West Twelfth Street between Sixth and Seventh. The closest, and Miss Holmes's hard luck if she was still asleep.

A four-story building, a good deal like that on Washington Place in which Janet Rushton had lived and died. Another converted one-family house. Two apartments to the floor, here. And—yes—Stacey Holmes. On the fourth floor, from the location of the bell push. It would be.

He pressed the button and, after some seconds, a voice came out of a grating. It rasped out of the grating. It did not sound like a singer's voice, but through these house-phone gadgets voices never sounded much like voices, contralto or other. They sounded, at best, as if they came from badly scratched phonograph records. This voice said, "Yes? Who is it?"

Tony said, "Miss Holmes?" into the grating and got another "Yes," and, again, "Who is it?"

"My name's Cook," Tony said into the grating. "A police detective. Like a couple of words with you."

"What about?"

"This choir you've been singing in," Tony said. "Shouldn't take but a few minutes. Just a routine matter, Miss Holmes."

"It's awfully early," the voice said and, unexpectedly, it sounded like a voice. Apartment-to-entry telephones are cranky, with ways of their own—moody things. "I'm not dressed. But —oh, all right. Except I'm supposed to be uptown by ten-thirty."

Tony started to say that she'd have plenty of time to make it, but the latch clattered at him and he pushed his way in and climbed three flights of stairs and rang a doorbell. It was some seconds before he heard heels click behind the door. The door opened to the extent of a safety chain.

She was a small girl and looked very young. She had blonde hair and she was dressed, swaddled, in a quilted robe. But she had had time to put a face on. Probably, Tony thought, while he was climbing three flights of stairs. She looked up at him and said, "How do I know you're a detective? A girl's got to be careful."

"Should be, Miss Holmes," Tony said, and took his badge out of his pocket and held it out so that she could see it. She looked at it with care. If Janet Rushton had been half as cautious—

"I guess it's all right," Stacey Holmes said. "A girl down this way let somebody in and he killed her. A girl I *knew*. Sort of knew, anyway. It's—well, I guess it's made everybody jumpy."

"Reason to be jumpy," Tony said. "More people ought to be." He put his badge back in his pocket and she unhooked the chain, and he went into the apartment. It was one large room, with windows on the street side. Just inside the door a closet jutted into the room, and it had slatted doors, closed. Kitchen facilities, Tony thought. Or what perhaps was called a kitchenette. On the other side there was another walled area bulging into the room. The door to this was solid. Bathroom. A narrow passage between them into the big room. The room was long and there were bright pictures on the walls, and the daybed had been made up. And sun came in through the tall windows at the room's end.

Stacey Holmes walked ahead of him into the room. The

quilted robe bundled around her. But underneath it, Tony thought, she probably was slender and neatly put together. And she was a blonde. Would have made a suitable guide for the Reverend Jonathan Prentis? He had preferred blondes, if they could take Farmington's word for it. If they could take Farmington's word for anything.

The girl sat on the made-up day bed. But then she bounced off it and said, "I was just going to have coffee. You want some coffee?"

"I guess not," Tony said, but then, "Coffee would be fine, Miss Holmes."

He went to one of the tall windows and looked down into Twelfth Street. Nothing much was going on in Twelfth Street, except that the harsh wind was blowing loose papers through it. The wind had knocked over an empty trash can, and it rolled a little way with the wind and brought up against another trash can and stopped.

The girl brought a tray with two filled cups from the kitchen closet and put it down on a table. She said, "There isn't any cream. Cream is fattening."

"I don't take cream," Tony said, and sat where he could reach the cup and tasted the coffee. Instant, but pretty good instant. He said, "You make good coffee, Miss Holmes," and she said, "Out of a jar, but it's easier. What do you want to ask me, mister—what did you say your name was?"

Tony told her again what his name was. He said, "This girl who got killed. The girl you sort of knew. Janet Rushton?"

"Yes," Stacey said. "That's the one. She was—we were—in this choir. The Voice's—*oh!*"

"Yes," Tony said. "He got killed too."

She said, "Oh," again. She said, "I don't know anything about it. About either of them. Why would I?"

"No reason," Tony told her. "We don't think you do. We're just—oh, just poking around, the way we have to. You were in the choir with Miss Rushton. Knew her. We're trying to find out everything we can about her."

"Not all that well I didn't know her," the girl said. She got a pack of cigarettes out of a pocket of the quilted robe and looked at it and shook her head at it and then said, "Got a match?" Tony snapped his lighter for her and held it across the small table. He got a cigarette out of his own pocket and lighted it.

"Just to say hello to," Stacey said and sipped from her cup. "There were an awful lot of us. She was in a show for a while. Had a number. But I didn't really know her. She was blonde, like me, and she wore green a lot. She had one green dress that must have cost her—wow! Square neckline and a yellow stripe going across from one shoulder, diagonally, you know, and—"

"Yes," Tony said. "I'm sure she dressed well. She had an attractive apartment. But you didn't know her at all well, you say."

"Like I said," Stacey Holmes said, "there were a lot of us. Boys and girls. And when we put on those robe things you couldn't tell us apart. Not really."

"Did you know Mr. Prentis? Aside from who he was, I mean."

"He was pretty tremendous," the girl said. "That voice of his. Gave you the shivers, sort of. No. He didn't pay any attention to the girls in the choir. Mr. Farmington did that. Only not much, really. If you could carry a tune. That was about all he cared about."

"Any of the other girls know Mr. Prentis? To speak to, I mean? Miss Rushton, for example?"

"I wouldn't know," Stacey said. "Really I wouldn't. It was just a job. We lined up and marched out and sang hymns, and after it was over, we came home. It was—oh, just a way to pick up some change, if you know what I mean. There aren't all that many jobs going around. Reason I've got to be uptown at ten-thirty, my agent thinks maybe he's got something lined up for me. Anyway, somebody's casting. Supposed to open next September, but who knows?"

"For singing in the choir," Tony said. "Fifty dollars a performance? That right?"

"It's what they sent the agents," she said. "At least, far's I know we all got the same. Fifty I got. Less Joe's cut. Joe Westclock, that is. He's Talent, Incorporated."

"Ten per cent, that would have been? His cut?"

"Yes," Stacey Holmes said. "Only then there was the tithing. Only it wasn't, really. Not the way it worked out, because it was off the top."

Tony Cook shook his head. He finished his coffee and shook his head again and said he didn't get it.

"Well," the girl said, "it was new to me. Called that, anyway. A tenth, it means, he said. It's a religious term, I guess. Anyway, it was, the way he put it, to help carry on the work. Work of—what was the word he used? Redemp-something. Oh, I remember. Redemption."

"You—each of you—were supposed to pay back a tenth of what you got?" Tony said. "As a contribution to the—the mission? That would be—let's see—four dollars for each time you sang?"

"Five dollars," Stacey Holmes said. "You didn't listen. I said it was off the top. Fifty dollars was the top."

"You all did this—tithing?"

"Sure. It was part of getting the job. Joe said that was the way it was set up. The way it always was. He said it was the way Mr. Farmington wanted it because, he guessed, Mr. Farmington was a very religious man and thought everybody ought to contribute. Only Joe said, 'To the Second Coming, I gather.' He makes jokes like that. But he said we had to take it or leave it, and forty dollars is—well, it only took a couple of hours, you know. And it was three times a week. And you could take other jobs the other nights. If you could get them."

Tony put his cigarette out. But almost at once, looking across the table at the bundled-up girl, he lighted another.

"They're bad for you," the girl said. "Do things to your voice. My teacher keeps telling me that, and I'm down to five a day. Most days, anyway."

"Probably your teacher's right," Tony said. "This five dollars. This tithe. The agency take it out of your check?"

"No, it wasn't that way. When we showed up to be checked in—Mr. Farmington did that himself—we got little envelopes. With 'The Mission of Redemption, Inc.' printed on them. And we were supposed to put a five-dollar bill in them—or five ones, of course, but I usually put a five because sometimes taxi drivers can't change fives and they mostly won't at change booths." She stopped, with the finality of one who has made everything clear.

"After you put the money in the envelopes," Tony said, "you—what did you do with the envelopes?"

"Wrote our names on them and put them in the box," Stacey said. "It just said 'Contributions' on the box. It was on the table next to the one Mr. Farmington sat at when he checked us in."

"And?"

"I don't know what you mean by 'and,' " the girl said. "We put those robes on and lined up the way we were supposed to. I don't know what you mean by 'and.' "

"The box marked 'Contributions,' " Tony said. "Somebody took it away? One of the—ushers, or whatever they called them."

"I guess so," the girl said. "No, wait a minute. I was late once—not really late, but everybody was lining up. Maybe I was the last. I remember now. Mr. Farmington had a briefcase sort of thing under his table and when I'd checked in and put my envelope in the box, he started to take the envelopes out of the box and put them in this briefcase. Because they would be safer there, I guess. Because you don't just let money lie around loose, do you?"

Mr. Ralph Farmington didn't, Tony thought. But all he said was, "It isn't a good idea to let money lie around loose."

The girl pulled back the quilted sleeve of her robe and looked at the watch on her wrist. She said, "It's pretty near ten and I've got to dress and be uptown by—"

"Yes," Tony said, and looked at his own watch. "You will have to hurry, Miss Holmes. I'm sorry I kept you so long."

But, again on the sidewalk, walking toward the next on his list, Tony Cook wasn't really sorry. He did hope the girl would make it and that she'd get a job in the show which, perhaps, was going to open in September. He wished the small blonde girl well. She had been a help.

By noon, when he had made his last call—a call in Gay Street—Tony had something to take back to the headquarters of Homicide South. He had the names and addresses of six girl singers and two men who had paid kickbacks for their jobs in the choir of Mission of Redemption, Inc. Oh, all right, what looked like being kickbacks. Call the payments tithes if you want to.

Since he was in Gay Street and it was lunchtime, he pushed a button under a name in the entry hall of a small apartment house. The bell rang on the second floor and he could hear it ringing. But it wasn't answered.

Well, he hadn't really expected it would be. He went, by subway, up to Twentieth Street.

10

Shapiro got to West Twentieth Street at a little after nine that Friday morning and, briefly, shuffled papers. The full post-mortem report on Janet Rushton was in. It added nothing to the preliminary report, except that she had not been pregnant. She had not been raped. Her fingerprints had been checked out. A few years previously she had been licensed as a cabaret performer, at a time when all employees of restaurants with entertainment had been fingerprinted. So, she was Janet Rushton. She had been born in Hot Springs, Arkansas, which is not too far from Little Rock. Which was somewhat interesting, but neither suggested nor proved anything. She had been the oldest of three daughters of Dr. and Mrs. Robert E. L. Rushton. Her parents were living and had been notified.

Mr. and Mrs. Jonathan Prentis had been married ten years before in Springfield, Missouri. Neither had been previously married. Her age had been given as "over twenty-one."

Bits and pieces.

Captain William Weigand was in his office. Asked by Weigand, Nathan Shapiro said that, so far as he could see, things weren't coming at all. He said that the people involved were, as usual, people he was incapable of understanding. He said, "Look, Bill, it's nothing to grin at." He said, "Usually it doesn't make any difference and we both know it. But this is the sort of thing a Christian would be better at. Maybe a Christian—a Protestant Christian anyway—would be able to sort these people out." He said that, probably, the Reverend Prentis had been playing around with a girl in the choir—the girl who was dead now. He said that, probably, a man named Farmington had given Prentis a lead on girls. He said that Tony Cook had got the notion that Farmington was taking kickbacks from the men and women he hired, locally, for the choir and that Tony was now checking it out. He said, "Oh, all right, I'm the wrong man for it, but all right." He said he was going back up to the hotel and talk some more to the people who made up the mission.

"Money?" Weigand said. "There've been stories about Prentis's setup. That a lot of people have contributed a lot of money."

"Money is the root of all evil," Shapiro said. He shook his head sadly. "Probably from the Bible," he said.

"It is," Bill Weigand told him. "Oh, it's 'The love of money is the root of all evil.' But it's from the New Testament, Nate, I think."

Nathan Shapiro, his gloomiest expectations justified, got a car from the pool and went uptown to the Hotel Wexley. He found Ralph Farmington talking into the telephone in the living room of the suite he shared with the Reverend John Wesley Higgs. He was talking in a hushed voice. As Shapiro went in he said, "O.K., Joe. You can put it that way. Looks like I am or will be. So if anything—"

Farmington did not finish the sentence, Shapiro thought because he had come into the room. Farmington put the receiver back in its cradle, very gently. He gestured toward the door of Higgs's room. He got up from the desk and came around it and edged Shapiro toward the door.

"Trying to get some sleep, Higgs is," Farmington said, in what was not quite a whisper. "Didn't get in until after three, he and Pruitt didn't."

"All right," Shapiro said. "It's Mrs. Prentis I'd like to see now. If she's up to it. Happen to know whether she is?"

Farmington said he didn't. He said Mrs. Mathews had pretty much taken over as far as Mrs. Prentis was concerned. Asked, he said that, yes, Henry Pruitt was staying at the hotel with the rest of them; that he had moved into the room Prentis had occupied and that this captain whatever-his-name-was had said it was all right.

"Perfectly all right," Shapiro told him. "We've picked up anything in the room we thought might help."

Maloney was a good cop, and Shapiro could be sure that had been done. And reasonably sure nothing of value had come of it—nothing, say, like a letter from somebody threatening to kill the Reverend Mr. Prentis. Shapiro went along the corridor to the suite occupied by Mrs. Florence Mathews and her assistants.

Mrs. Mathews was wearing a black dress. She was signing checks and sliding them across the desk to a middle-aged woman, also in a black dress, who was putting them in envelopes. When Shapiro went into the office room of the suite, Mrs. Mathews looked up and said, "Well?" and sounded angry about it. Then she said, "I haven't any time to waste this morning. There are a hundred things—"

"I'm sure there are," Shapiro said. "It's Mrs. Prentis I'd like to see for a few minutes. Mr. Farmington said to speak to you about it."

"Have you no respect? No consideration for one so recently bereaved?"

"A great deal," Shapiro said. "Also, I'm a policeman. Investigating a murder. Is she still under sedation? If the doctor says she can't be talked to—well, I'll have to wait till she can. Otherwise—"

"The doctor hasn't been in to see her this morning. There isn't anything she can tell you. You—you just want to persecute her. She's a gentle Christian woman who has suffered a great loss. She should be spared—"

"Mrs. Mathews," Shapiro said, and talked like a policeman, "I have no intention of persecuting Mrs. Prentis. But I have every intention of seeing her. Now, if she's up to it. You've probably seen her this morning, haven't you?"

"Of course. She is afflicted. It is no more than my duty. I persuaded her to let me order a little breakfast sent up. She must keep up her strength."

"Of course," Shapiro said. "Very wise of you, Mrs. Mathews. She's up and dressed, I take it? The sedation's worn off?"

"Well—"

"So," he said, "I'll try to be as brief as I can. As considerate."

He turned back toward the door. Mrs. Mathews started to get up from the desk.

"No," Shapiro said. "You needn't come with me. I'm not going to persecute Mrs. Prentis."

Mrs. Mathews continued to get up from the desk. She shook her head and started to walk around the desk.

"No," Shapiro said. He made it a very final "No." He went out of the room and closed the door after him. He went the length of the corridor and knocked at a door. A voice—rather a small and distant voice—said, "Who is it?" and Shapiro told Mrs. Jonathan Prentis who it was. There was a pause of some seconds, and then she said, "The door isn't locked."

It was a corner room, with windows on two sides. There was a waiter's cart in the middle of it and used dishes on the cart. Mrs. Prentis had had eggs for breakfast, and had eaten them. Also bacon. She was keeping up her strength.

She sat in a chair by one of the windows and had a book open on her lap. The Bible, Shapiro saw when he had partly crossed the room. A Bible in limp-leather binding. The hands on the Bible were shapely but, for a woman's, rather large. She was blonde and, Shapiro thought, on the whole good-looking—all of her large and shapely. And younger than he had expected her to be. She wore a black dress. He did not think she had been crying, and she seemed quite composed.

She said, "I told the young woman yesterday all I have to tell." She said, "It is nothing. Was nothing. Only someone very evil could have harmed my husband. They say he was in an evil place when it happened. He had gone to seek out evil. To strive against it. He was a man of God."

"There are one or two things you may be able—"

"I seek consolation in the Word of God," she said. She lifted up the Bible. "The inspired Word." The capitalization was in her voice. It was a light, assured voice and, Shapiro thought, one without warmth. "Are you a Christian, Lieutenant?"

"No," Shapiro said. "Of another faith."

She merely nodded her head.

Shapiro pulled a chair up and sat on it, facing her.

"The usual question," he said. "Do you know of anyone who might have had reason—thought he had reason—to harm your husband? An enemy?"

"He had no enemies. He was a friend of all men, even of those who sinned. If you had known him, you would not have asked that question."

"Probably," Shapiro said. "But I didn't know him. And someone killed him. We're trying to find out who killed him."

"A hand guided by Satan. A soul corrupted by evil. Is not that enough?"

"No," Shapiro said. "I'm afraid it isn't. We have to be more —specific. There's nobody you suspect, then?"

"No one. He was greatly loved. He was—"

"Yes," Shapiro said. "I realize he was a man of God." And God knows I ought to by now, Shapiro thought. "Night before last, you didn't see your husband? After the meeting, I mean. When he came back here and changed and went out again?"

"No. I was sleeping. Florence persuaded me to take sleeping medicine. I had a very bad cold and had not been sleeping."

"Bad time of year for colds," Shapiro said. "Better now?"

She said, "Yes," and then, a little to Nathan's surprise, added, "Thank you."

"I realize this is difficult for you," Shapiro said. "I'm trying to keep it as brief as I can. But there's routine, you see. Things we have to go through, whether they mean anything or not. Did Mr. Prentis often go out into a city to—to assess its wickedness—before the meetings started?"

This is getting to me, Shapiro thought. I'm beginning to talk like these people; stilted, as they talk. Pretty soon I'll begin quoting from the Bible. Or the Talmud. What little I remember of what they taught me at *schule*.

"I knew he sometimes went in search of evil. That he might destroy it. He did not shirk his duty."

Shapiro said he was sure the Reverend Mr. Prentis had not shirked his duty.

"He saw things which made him cringe," Mrs. Prentis said. "He faced such things."

"Sure," Nathan said, lapsing into more comfortable speech. "There's one small thing we'd like to get straightened out. Nothing important, but we try to get everything tucked in."

She looked at him. She had rather light blue eyes. They were eyes he couldn't see into. But he was never any good at seeing into the eyes of others.

"You came east with the others," he said. "In a chartered

plane on the second of this month. That's what we're told, anyway."

"Yes."

"But you left Little Rock on the twenty-second of last month. That was a Sunday. Flew to Saint Louis. That's right, isn't it?"

"I try not to fly on Sunday," she said. "To do anything on Sunday. Remember the Sabbath Day to keep it holy."

"Yes," Shapiro said. "But you did fly to Saint Louis on a Sunday. And stayed there until the second of this month, when you flew here with the others?"

"It was a day I could get a seat on the plane. Saturday was booked solidly, they told me."

"It was urgent that you get to Saint Louis?"

"Urgent? No. Why should it be urgent? I was merely lonely in Little Rock. We have quite a large house there. Next to the Tabernacle."

"Your brother lives in Saint Louis," Shapiro said. "You—I suppose you flew up to visit him before coming on east with the others?"

"I saw my brother, certainly."

"Of course," Shapiro said. "Natural thing to do. Stayed with him until it was time to fly to New York? He's here now, by the way. But of course you know that."

"I knew he was expected. Somebody told me his plane was delayed. Florence told me he had arrived and—and had been very late. And is sleeping now."

"Yes," Shapiro said. "I'll probably want to see him when he wakes up. But there's no hurry. In Saint Louis during that week or so. You did stay with your brother?"

"Does it matter? How can it matter?"

"Probably doesn't at all. We just have to fill things in. Things that don't make any difference one way or another. But, you did stay with him?"

"No. I went into a retreat. For prayer and meditation. Often I do before the meetings begin. To prepare myself to hold up his hands. To minister to his needs."

"A retreat?"

"A place in which to withdraw from the world. We—the mission—have several of them throughout the country. Many—the wives of our ministers, sometimes our returned missionaries—go to them to—to commune with God."

"Of course," Nathan said. "Heard of such places, of course. Thought they were mostly Roman Catholic. Or Episcopalian, sometimes."

"Ours are not like theirs," she said. "We follow the simple way. The true way. We make no graven images. Do not pollute our air with incense. We follow in the footsteps of the Master."

Shapiro said he understood, which was not especially true. He said, "This retreat you went to. In Saint Louis?"

"No. Here in the east. In a place called North White Plains."

"Flew here to this retreat? Then back to Saint Louis to fly back with the rest?"

"Yes. Is that so strange? My place is with the others. My modest place."

It seemed strange enough to Nathan Shapiro. Except, of course, that North White Plains is a short train ride from Grand Central Terminal. If a wife wants to check up on her husband who has—how had she put it?—has gone in search of evil. "That he might destroy it." All Nathan said was "Mmmm," which was not especially conclusive.

"When he came back from the meeting night before last," Shapiro said, "Mr. Prentis did not—oh, look in on you? To see that you were all right? How you were making out with this bad cold?"

"I told you I was sleeping. Sleeping deeply because of this medicine. If he did, he didn't wake me up."

"Probably did," Shapiro said. "Saw you were sleeping. Didn't want to waken you. Sort of thing a man might do, I'd think."

She did not say anything to that.

"Because," Shapiro said, "you and your husband were close, I imagine. Been married ten years, I understand. Time draws people together."

Or, of course, pushes them apart.

"We were married," she said. "Together in holy matrimony. In the sight of God."

"Of course," Shapiro said. She sounded, he thought, a little sharp about it. Which wasn't—at any rate he supposed wasn't—any of his business. He said, "I'm sorry, Mrs. Prentis. I realize all this must be difficult for you. My—my prying into the past. Stirring up memories which must be dear to you."

She sighed deeply for answer. And, Shapiro found, he did not in the least believe in her sigh. Which somewhat surprised him. She sighed again, and he did not believe that sigh either.

"We were spiritually as one," she said. "We were dedicated together to the service of our Lord."

Shapiro thought for a moment and then repeated, "Spiritually?" He resisted the temptation to quote from the Scriptures himself, "Male and female created He them."

"Of course," Mrs. Hope Prentis said. "We did not sin together."

He could only repeat the word "Sin?" He repeated it with a rising inflection.

"Carnally," she said. "We had put all that behind us, of course."

Shapiro said he was afraid he did not quite understand.

"I can have no children," she said. "I am a barren woman. A year after we were married I learned that from a doctor. Why do I tell you this? It can have no connection."

Shapiro was not so sure of that. A woman who has abandoned sex, if that was what Mrs. Prentis was edging her way around, is not likely to experience sexual jealousy. Bluntly, to kill a husband who is playing around with another blonde.

"No," Nathan said. "It can have no connection, of course. I hadn't intended to bring up such a—a delicate subject. You could have no children. And so you—you and Mr. Prentis didn't—" He hesitated, rejecting certain words. "You and Mr. Prentis remained continent?" he said. "With each other?"

"Of course," she said. "Our relationship was chaste. If children cannot be expected, it is only sin. Lasciviousness. The employment of the bodies given us by God for carnal pleasure. After we knew, we did not sin."

Shapiro had been puzzled by these people from the start. He felt now that there was an enormity in this hotel room. He stood up rather suddenly and said, "Thank you, Mrs. Prentis. I'm sorry to have had to bother you at a time like this," and got out of the room.

He thought of Rose and of how they had clung together when they first heard that, together, they could not have children. And of how they had clung together since. He felt he was leaving an enormity behind him in the corner room of the Hotel Wexley.

A waiter was bringing a tray with used dishes on it out of the room across the hall—the room which had been the Reverend Prentis's. Henry Pruitt was awake, apparently, and had had breakfast. Shapiro knocked at his door. A man behind the door said, "Come back later, can't you?" in a resonant voice. He spoke as one might speak to a maid come too early to straighten a room.

"A police officer, Mr. Pruitt," Shapiro said through the door. "Like a few words with you."

Pruitt did not answer. But Shapiro heard a bolt slide and then the door opened.

Pruitt was a tall man and a heavy one. He was fully dressed —dark gray suit, with vest; white shirt and a black four-in-hand necktie. Except for the fact that he was wearing slippers, he was a man ready to go to an office and take charge. He didn't, Shapiro thought with some relief, look like a particularly religious man. He had blue eyes which were rather like his sister's.

"Lieutenant Shapiro," Shapiro said. "One of those investigating Mr. Prentis's death."

"Terrible thing," Pruitt said. "Unbelievable. I was in Saint Louis. Nothing I can tell you."

"I don't suppose there is," Shapiro said. "But they want us to talk to everybody."

The unidentified "they" is often useful.

"Only take a few minutes," Shapiro added. "Realize you'll have a lot to do. Getting things straightened out. Or, will it be wound up?"

"Nothing I can tell you," Pruitt said again. "Nobody's safe in a city like this. Criminals let run loose. Probably some homicidal maniac you people have let go."

He started to pull the door closed. Nathan Shapiro held it

open. For a moment they looked at each other. Then Pruitt said, "Oh, come on in. You'll be wasting time. Nothing I can tell you."

But he went on into the corner room, which was identical, in reverse, of the one occupied by his sister across the hall. Pruitt sat down, solidly, in a chair, a man who had no time to waste, who wanted to get on with it.

"Assuming it wasn't a homicidal maniac," Shapiro said, "who would gain by Mr. Prentis's death?"

"Nobody. Oh, anybody who wanted to stop his work. A fanatic atheist. Good many of those around. Stopped prayers in schools, people like that did. In a God-fearing country. Breaking down the moral fiber. Part of the conspiracy. Communist. Somebody like that it could have been."

Easy enough to place now, Shapiro thought. Not religious in the sense the others were. But with his own religion. Member of the Birch Society, probably. He'd heard they were strong out west.

"Yes," Shapiro said. "It could have been somebody like that, I suppose. If it was, we'll find him. But what I was wondering about was a personal motive. Or, of course, a financial motive. We have to look for that sort of thing."

"Won't find it," Pruitt told him. "What do you mean, financial?"

"I don't know," Shapiro said. "I'm trying to find out. You're treasurer of the Mission of Redemption. From what I've heard about it, a great deal of money is involved. We always wonder when a great deal of money is involved."

"No," Pruitt said. "People are always trying to find out about that. Reporters. Magazine writers. Nobody's business. Nonprofit religious corporation. Tax-exempt. Jonathan's death won't have anything to do with that. Not with what's in the treasury now, anyway."

"With what may come in?"

"All right. The cause will suffer, if that's what you're getting at."

"Somebody will take Mr. Prentis's place. Carry on his work?"

"Look. This just happened. We haven't got to planning anything. Higgs and I, and Mrs. Mathews—it'll be up to us, I suppose. All I can tell you now is we've canceled the Chicago meetings. After that—"

He shrugged heavy shoulders.

"Mr. Higgs himself? I understand he helped Mr. Prentis. Helped him write sermons. Syndicate articles. That sort of thing? He might take Mr. Prentis's place?"

"Listen," Pruitt said. "Probably you people have talked to the Reverend Higgs. Heard him talk?"

"Yes."

"Jonathan was a dedicated man," Pruitt said. "A man of God. Also—you know what we called him? The Voice. Listening to him—well, it was an experience. When they listened to him, a lot of people thought God was speaking. Felt as if He were speaking. You've heard Pruitt's voice, you say. Well?"

"He did help Mr. Prentis with the writing? Higgs, I mean?"

"Sure. More than one man could handle. Even Jonathan. Doesn't mean he can take Jonathan's place. However dedicated he is."

"So, you don't know what will happen next?"

"The mission will continue, certainly. Our funds will be used as they have been to carry on the work. To send young men to study for the ministry. To support the retreats. To carry on the missionary work in heathen lands. To people who have not heard the Word. Our work is not ended. It will not be ended in our time."

"Probably not," Shapiro said. "Speaking of retreats. Place where people go to—to contemplate? To pray?"

"To find refuge," Pruitt said. "Widows of our clergy. Missionaries who have grown old in the work. Ministers who have worn themselves out in the service of the Lord."

"Many of these retreats supported by the Mission of Redemption?"

"Twenty-one. Throughout the country. Oh, mostly in the South. Where our greatest strength is, although we advance throughout the nation."

Partly businessman, Shapiro thought. Partly—partly what? Publicity man?

"Speaking of retreats," Shapiro said. "Your sister spent some time in one last month, she tells me. One quite close to New York."

"She often did," Pruitt said. "To prepare herself. She has always been invaluable as Jonathan's helpmeet. A splendid woman. A dedicated woman. She will bear her cross with courage."

Shapiro said he was sure she would. He asked a few more questions, but not about the financial setup of the Mission of Redemption, Inc. It was evident that on that subject Pruitt wasn't talking. Oh, the courts could intervene, if it came to that. As it might or might not.

Yes, Mrs. Prentis had flown from Little Rock to St. Louis late in February. She had stayed for a day or so with her brother. She had flown to New York and stayed for a time in the retreat and had flown back to St. Louis to come east again with the others.

Yes, Jonathan Prentis often went ahead of the others to a city where the meeeings were to be held, to familiarize himself with conditions. Evil took various forms; he wanted to be familiar with the most recent.

Yes, the retreat in North White Plains had an address. It was on a numbered route. Anybody could tell Lieutenant Shapiro where it was. It was called "Mission Retreat 14." All the retreats had numbers. What did the police want to know for?

"They want a lot of details," Shapiro said, and thanked Pruitt for giving him the time on what would be, of course, a busy morning.

Shapiro went out of the room and along the hall to the suite shared by Farmington and Higgs. There was nobody in it. He went down to the main floor and looked into the coffee shop. Higgs was there, having breakfast.

Shapiro got a taxi to Grand Central Station and had to wait almost half an hour for an express to White Plains and, beyond it, North White Plains. The train ended its run at North White Plains. It was only fifteen minutes late in getting there. There was a cab at the station and, sure, the driver knew where Mission Retreat 14 was. It was maybe five miles out in the country.

North White Plains was country enough for Nathan Shapiro,

who can take open spaces or leave them alone—preferably leave them alone if they are more open than Prospect Park. The country was a good deal more open to the east of North White Plains, but after a mile or so the cab warmed up. If one is going to chase wild geese, it is well to do it in a warm taxicab.

The taxi turned off a wide main road onto a narrower blacktop, with the winter's chuckholes in it. It went more slowly, dodging the holes. At a gravel drive with a sign beside it which read "Mission Retreat 14" the taxi slowed. "Maybe and maybe not," the driver said. "They fall apart this time of year. Frost goes out and they fall apart."

He turned into the drive, very slowly. Shapiro could feel the front wheels sink into it. The driver backed the taxi out and said, "Nope. Don't want to take the chance. Have to walk up, mister."

"Wait," Shapiro said. "I won't be long."

The driver said, "Well, mister—" and Shapiro looked at him.

"O.K.," the driver said. "I'll have to charge you extra. You know that, don't you?"

"Yes," Shapiro said. "I know that." He got out of the cab and began to walk.

11

The graveled drive went a hundred yards or so through a rough-mowed field toward a sprawling white house. It was mushy underfoot and there were puddles in it. Shapiro skirted the puddles, but his feet got wet all the same. The northwest wind whipped at him. It would dry up the puddles, given time. Or, on the other hand, freeze them. There was little warmth in the late March sun.

A covered porch stretched along the front of the rambling house, and wicker chairs, some of them rocking chairs, were tilted back against the house, waiting disconsolately for summer. Shapiro went up onto the porch, and his wet shoes left wet prints on the flooring. He looked for a doorbell and did not find one and knocked on the door. He had to knock several times before a sturdy middle-aged woman in a severe black dress opened it. She looked at him searchingly and with what appeared to be distrust.

"Police officer," Shapiro said. "From the city. This is a—one of the retreats of the Mission of Redemption?"

"What it says on the sign," the woman said. "I can't imagine what a policeman wants here."

"A couple of questions," Shapiro said. "About one of the people who stayed here late last month."

"The people who come here are God-fearing people," the woman said. "Nobody the police would want to ask questions about. They come here for peace." She paused for a moment. "And to pray," she said. "And you're letting cold air in. Hard enough to keep the place warm this time of year."

"If I come in," Shapiro said, "we can close the door."

She said, "Well," with doubt in her voice, but stepped aside, and Shapiro went into a large, bare hall. She closed the door after him. It was a little warmer inside, but not much. The retreat did not pamper its guests. He followed the sturdy woman into a room off the hall. It was a little warmer there. There were hard-looking chairs in the room and even a sofa. It looked as resolute as the chairs and as uninviting. The women walked —marched—to the sofa and sat on it. Shapiro had seen police matrons who were more yielding. The woman said, "Well?"

"Mind telling me your name?" Shapiro said.

"Brown, Mrs. Brown. Well?"

"About Mrs. Jonathan Prentis," Shapiro said. "You know her husband's dead? Was killed?"

"We've been told," she said and Shapiro waited for the inevitable. "He was a man of God," Mrs. Brown said. "But the forces of evil will not triumph. What about Mrs. Prentis? She is a saintly woman."

"We hear she was here for a time last month," Shapiro said. "That right?"

Mrs. Brown failed to see how it could concern the police. "People come to us to withdraw from the world," she said. "To contemplate and pray. It is a private matter. We do not discuss our guests."

"Mrs. Brown," Shapiro said, "Mrs. Prentis told me she came here. Late last month. She made no secret of it."

"Then why are you asking me?" the sturdy woman said. "If you know already. What's your name, by the way?"

Shapiro told her what his name was. She said, "Oh," with a certain inflection. She said, "From the New York City police?"

"Yes," Shapiro said. "Mr. Prentis was killed in New York. I'm one of those trying to find out who killed him. We have to check out on a lot of things. Ask a lot of questions which probably aren't important. Mrs. Prentis was here?"

"She came on the twenty-third," Mrs. Brown said. "She had come before when the Voice came to redeem the city. To prepare herself to be by his side in his great work. His vital work."

"Yes," Shapiro said. "How long did she stay this time?"

"From Monday to Saturday. Then she left here, refreshed, to rejoin her husband."

Shapiro briefly wondered whether it was here that Hope Prentis had caught her cold. He thought he probably would be catching one himself, with wet feet and everything.

"Left when?"
"The last of the month—the twenty-eighth."
"And went where?"
"I did not ask her. I assume to the city."
"Mrs. Brown, can you tell me how this place operates? How many come here? That sort of thing? I'm not familiar with—retreats of this kind."
Mrs. Brown said she assumed as much. She said it tartly.
"It is supported by the Mission of Redemption," Shapiro said, and made his sad voice patient. "That's right, isn't it? Are the, er, guests"—he realized he had almost said "Inmates"—"charged for their rooms? And, I assume, their food? And you are the—" he paused. "Wardress" seemed appropriate, but probably was not.
"Housekeeper," Mrs. Brown said. "No, there is no charge. It is a refuge for those who have spent their lives in the service of our Lord. And for others, like Mrs. Prentis herself, who come briefly to strengthen themselves by communion with their Maker."
Shapiro said he understood; that she had made it very clear. He said, "The guests here? Do they have visitors? Friends? Relatives?"
"Not often. They have withdrawn from worldly things. Are locked in contemplation and prayer."
"But they can have visitors?"
"Of course. This is not a prison."
"And can leave as they like? I mean for a few hours. A day or so, perhaps?"
"If they wish. Few of them do. They have come to—"
"Yes," Shapiro said. He felt he was now clear enough on that. "Did Mrs. Prentis have visitors while she was here? Or did she leave—to go to the city, perhaps—and return?"
"The Reverend Mr. Higgs came to see her. Twice, I think. No, she did not leave during the time she stayed here. It would have been necessary for me to call a taxicab for her if she had wished to leave."
"She couldn't have called one for herself?"
"There is only one telephone. In my office."
"And Mr. Higgs came twice to visit her?"

"The *Reverend* Mr. Higgs. Yes."

"She seem nervous while she was here? Upset? Anything like that?"

"Not in the least. She found tranquillity here."

"Not after Mr. Higgs visited her?"

"He is a man of God. Peace moves with him. Certainly not, Lieutenant Shapiro."

"Shapiro stood up and thanked her for her cooperation in the proper words and walked back down the hundred yards of mushy driveway. It hadn't dried out any. And this time he was walking against the harsh wind. He shivered as he walked.

The taxi driver had kept his motor running and the cab was warm. He also had his radio on. It sounded to Shapiro like the kind of music they played at the Village Brawl. The next train to New York was in half an hour, but not from North White Plains. From White Plains itself. They could just about make it, but he'd have to charge extra.

They did make it. He did charge extra. Shapiro would get the money back after the expense accounts were audited. And, of course, if his was approved. He couldn't see why it wouldn't be. A lot of errands policemen have to go on prove fruitless in the end.

The train was warm. Actually, the car he was in was hot. The train left White Plains station on time. For twenty minutes it ran briskly. Then it stopped. It did not stop at a station: it did not seem to have stopped for any particular reason. After about twenty minutes, a trainman walked through the car toward the rear. He did not appear to be concerned. He was polite when the woman in the seat ahead of Shapiro's asked what had happened.

"We're all right," the trainman said. "Nothing the matter with *this* train. One up ahead lost its shoes. Shouldn't be long, only maybe we'll have to push it in."

It was long, and they did have to push ahead of them the train which had managed to lose its third-rail shoes. They got to Grand Central some two hours late and it was after lunchtime, and Shapiro's stomach, which is usually cross, was furious. He got lunch in the Commodore Grill and had a drink before it. Not Sherry. Scotch on the rocks. He felt he had it coming, whatever his stomach might say about it.

He thought of Hope Prentis's strange confession. Or was it a strange boast? A strange and righteous boast? He thought of the visits the Reverend Higgs had made to the bleak retreat outside North White Plains and wondered if Higgs had come to bring news to Mrs. Prentis of her husband and his "guide." He thought that Mrs. Prentis had rather large hands, for a woman. Strong hands. Attached, he thought, to a strong woman.

He went cross-town by shuttle and downtown on the Seventh Avenue to Twenty-third Street and walked the rest of the way. The wind hadn't moderated or got warmer. In his office he took his shoes off and propped them against the radiator, which might dry them and would certainly stiffen them. He spread the papers from his In basket on the desk.

A carbon of Tony Cook's report was one of the papers. Eight members of the mission's choir had "tithed." Which seemed to Shapiro an odd way of putting it. Farmington had picked up the envelopes with the money in them. To add them to the general collections? He would say that, of course. It would, obviously, be difficult to prove he hadn't—to prove that "tithes" could be read as "kickbacks."

Tony had gone to call on more choir singers.

A hundred and eighty or so at five dollars a performance. No—a "gospel meeting." Came to nine hundred dollars a meeting, if there were a hundred and eighty each time and nobody said go take a flying. Three meetings a week. Twenty-seven hundred dollars a week. A reasonably substantial contribution to the conversion of the ungodly. Or, of course, to somebody. Back to the Hotel Wexley, of which Shapiro was thoroughly tired, for a talk with Ralph Farmington.

If a profitable kickback, had Prentis somehow got word of it? Had he threatened to fire Farmington? Or, conceivably, to turn him over to the police? Twenty-seven hundred a week. The engagement at the Garden had run three weeks. Shapiro needed pencil and paper. Eighty-one hundred. Make it *eight* thousand or thereabouts. Some of the singers might have been off sick from time to time. Or told Farmington to go roll his hoop.

He went on with the papers from the In basket. A good many of them had to do with other matters. There is never one case at a time at Homicide South. Some of the papers merely required initials, and got them. Some would need more, and those Shapiro laid aside. He made neat piles of papers. He came to a photograph.

It was of Janet Rushton, lying dead on her bed in her apartment. Except for the face, which did not look as it had looked, gay and smiling, on the glossies provided by her agent, the dead girl looked like a quietly sleeping girl. She lay on her back.

She wore a dress; what seemed to Nathan Shapiro a pretty dress. Not one of those with miniskirts. This dress came well below her knees, as she lay dead. It lay smooth over her knees, and her knees were close together, touching each other. It was almost, he thought, as if her clothes had been arranged to make a pretty picture.

But that was ridiculous. Police photographers do not seek pretty pictures. She had been lying so, so neatly, when she had been found. Or had the men who found her straightened her clothes? He thought back to Tony Cook's report on that. No, according to Arthur Minor, who had come to take a girl to dinner and found her dead, she had been lying so—lying so peacefully, so neatly clothed—when he had first seen her dead.

But people do not die peacefully. With a pillow over a face, air gulped for, darkness fought against, people struggle. They writhe and fight to live, as all animals fight to live. They throw themselves around in attempt to escape the blackness. They tear at the hands which press the pillow down; tear at whatever hands can reach. They fight for life with hands and arms and legs. Clothing is, of course, deranged.

And this girl lay dead so neatly. So—the word came to Shapiro—so "properly." So—modestly.

The telephone rang on Shapiro's desk and he said, "Lieutenant Shapiro," into it. It still was rather an effort to say "Lieutenant."

"Cook; Nate. I've got seven more who chipped in. One who said he told Farmington to go to hell. But I doubt whether he really did. Shacking up with one of the girl singers, way it looks, and being big strong man. Want me to go on checking them out, or have we got enough?"

"Enough for now," Shapiro said. "We'll get Farmington to tell us about it tomorrow."

"He'll say they were voluntary contributions to carry on God's work," Tony Cook said. "Something like that."

"Yes," Shapiro said. "That's what he'll say. We'll listen. Meanwhile, a couple of men I'd like you to see. The men who found Janet Rushton's body. Minor, one of them was. And a man named—gone out of my mind. Owns the building she lived in."

"Brady," Cook told him. "Clifford Brady. Arthur Minor. Why?"

"I've been looking at a shot of her," Shapiro said. "All very neat. Dress smoothed down. Want to be sure Minor and Brady didn't smooth it down. Make her all decent. Because she wouldn't have been, I'd think. Because she would have struggled."

"She was slugged," Tony said. "Probably unconscious."

"I know. Knocked out, or pretty much out. And picked up and carried to her bed. And laid out neat and proper? And then smothered? I don't buy it, Tony. She died of asphyxiation, not of the blow on her jaw. There'd have been a reaction when the pillow went over her face."

"Yeah," Tony said. "You'd think she'd have fought back. Flounced around anyway. I'll check them out about it."

"Do that," Shapiro said. "And give me a ring at home. I went up to the country and got my feet wet. I'm probably coming down with a cold."

"Take something for it," Tony Cook said and hung up.

Shapiro sat for several moments waiting to sneeze. He didn't sneeze. He would, he thought morosely. Any time now he'd begin to sneeze.

He looked up a number in the Manhattan directory and dialed it and got, "Talent, Incorporated, good afternoon. Can I help you?"

"Mr. Westclock, please," Shapiro said, and got, "One moment, please," and then a male voice and "Westclock here," with an intonation which sounded English.

"Lieutenant Shapiro. Police Department. Mr. Ralph Farmington a client of yours, Mr. Westclock?"

"Well," Westclock said, and for seconds nothing further. Then he said, "Well," again. Then he said, "Ralph been up to something?"

"Routine," Shapiro told him. "In connection with the Prentis case."

"Don't figure Ralph's the type to stick ice picks in people," Westclock said. The British intonation had gone away. "However. Must cooperate with the police, what?" The intonation had returned. "Yes. Few weeks ago, he was collecting talent. For this choir he ran. But now he's back in my stable."

"Looking for an engagement?"

"Yes. But I don't know. Didn't tell him, of course, but he's a little past it, I'm afraid. Still got an all-right voice. But I don't know. No great demand for middle-aged baritones at the moment. I didn't tell him that, and it could be I'm wrong. Hope I am."

"But he is on your list. In your stable, as you put it. Looking for work?"

"As of yesterday. Because the revival racket's folded up on him, or he figures it has."

"Did you get him his job with the Mission of Redemption, Incorporated?"

"With the what?"

"What they call it," Shapiro said. "The people he was running the choir for."

"Oh," Westclock said. "The revival racket. No. And my percentage of quite a wad down the drain. I don't know how he latched onto that. Word around he went to one of these prayer meetings years back and got converted and talked them into letting him organize a choir. I wouldn't know."

"Got converted so he could get the job?"

"Now," Westclock said, "I didn't say that, Lieutenant. Be slander or something, wouldn't it? Far's I know Ralph's an all-right guy and a pretty good singer and, as of now, he's in my stable. See what I mean?"

Shapiro said yes, he saw what Mr. Westclock meant, and thanked Mr. Westclock for his help and put the receiver in its cradle. He looked at his watch. It was a little after four. In theory he was on the eight-to-four shift. He decided that, for once, fact and theory might conform and put his shoes on. They were still wet, but they had begun to stiffen up a little.

Nathan Shapiro got a subway train to Brooklyn, missing the worst of the rush hour. As he walked the Brooklyn streets it was still cold and blustery. But he still hadn't sneezed. Of course, colds take a while to incubate. Twenty-four hours or thereabouts, he thought it was.

He could have picked up Mrs. Jonathan Prentis's cold, the more quickly because he had got his feet wet. On the other hand, Mrs. Prentis's cold hadn't seemed at all bad—not any longer in the infectious stage. And she had big hands for a woman. Probably strong hands. He wondered whether, when she was younger, she had played games. Tennis, perhaps. It didn't seem likely. Probably religious people—very religious people; religious fanatics was what it came to—didn't play games. Probably it was sinful to play games. The use of God-given bodies for bodily enjoyment.

He stopped at a newsstand, and the blind news dealer said, "Afternoon, Lieutenant. It's sure getting colder," and Shapiro picked up a copy of the *Post*. He didn't have the exact change and handed a quarter to the news dealer. It didn't matter; change was almost instant in his hand. Fingers learn what eyes can no longer see.

"Police Link Slayings." As was to be expected. The police also anticipated an arrest. Which was only to be hoped for.

Shapiro climbed the one flight to his apartment and let himself in, and Rose was home already and all the lights were on, and the coils glowed in the fireplace. She wore a deep red housecoat, so she had been home for some time. She came to him and looked up at him and said, "*Nathan,*" in a certain way.

"All right," he told her. "Perfectly all right. I had to go up to the country and I got my feet wet."

"You're going to take a long hot bath," she told him. "Not just a shower. A long soak."

"All right," Nathan told his wife.

"And two Bufferin."

"Yes, dear."

"And really hot. And just lie in it."
"Yes, darling."
"Because it's bad to get your feet wet when you're tired."
"Mmmm."

It was fine to stretch out the length of the tub in hot water and, as it cooled, turn the hot on again with the toes. He had lain in hot water for fifteen minutes when the telephone rang. Rose said, "Lie still. I'll get it," through the bathroom door, and he could hear her footsteps as she crossed the room. He turned more hot water on with his toes.

She opened the door and went into the bathroom and looked at him stretching the length of the tub.

"Tony Cook," she said. "He said neither of them rearranged her clothes. And is there something else you want him to do before he knocks off for the day?"

"They both agree?"

"That's what Tony said."

"Tell him to call it a day."

"Which is what you're going to call it," Rose Shapiro said. "And when you're through soaking just put a robe on, and tonight you're going to have a real drink. Medicinal."

"But at lunch I had a—"

"Nathan."

"Yes, dear. A real drink."

When he went back into the living room, with a robe belted over pajamas, she had bottles and glasses and ice on a coffee table between sofa and fire. She had not mixed her own martini. She had put ice in her cocktail glass to chill it. His real drink was to be Scotch. She looked up at him and looked at him carefully and said, "Much better, darling. You look like somebody in the movies. I don't remember who."

"Clark Gable, probably," Nathan told her. "A very morose Clark Gable without a mustache. Made up to play the melancholy Dane."

"In a dressing gown," she said, and put ice in her mixing glass and in his stubby glass. She poured Scotch on the ice in his glass, even after he had said, "Whoa!" She mixed her martini and spilled the ice from her glass back into the ice container and measured gin and vermouth into the mixer and stirred and poured in her glass and twisted a sliver of lemon peel over it and rubbed the peel around the edge of the glass. She said, "There," and he stretched his legs out toward the electric coils in the fireplace, although he wasn't cold any longer. Come to think of it, he wasn't tired any longer, and he no longer expected to sneeze at any moment.

For some minutes they sat so and sipped their drinks. Scotch didn't taste as good to Nathan as his usual sweet wine. But it was warming. And his stomach had not protested—well, not actively protested—his drink before lunch. Those people up at the hotel are driving me to drink, Nathan thought, but he thought it without resentment.

"If you smother somebody with a pillow," Nathan said, "the person being smothered struggles. Fights."

"I would, certainly," Rose said. "I'd take it hard. 'Shrieking to the south and clutching at the north.' "

"Yes," he said. "And if you had clothes on they'd be—oh, heaped on you. Skirt up around your waist, because you'd kick to stay alive. Your legs every which way."

"Yes, Nathan. I'd think so. The girl who was with Prentis?"

"We think was with Prentis. Just before he was killed. Yes. Her clothes were very smooth. Very—seemly. If that's the word I want."

"It's a good word. An old word but a good word. I take it you mean—oh, decently covered."

"As if she were laid out," Nathan said. "Her dress smoothed down over her knees."

"Hands crossed on her chest?"

"No," he said. "Not that far. Straight down by her sides. She was that way when she was found, Rose. The men who found her are sure of that. What Tony called to tell me."

She nodded her head. She sipped from her glass.

"I don't understand these people," he said. "I think one of them killed Prentis and the girl. I can't prove it, and I don't know why. But I think somebody smothered the girl and smoothed her clothing down so that she would be, as you put it, decently covered. Who would do a thing like that, Rose?"

"I don't know. A man? Or a woman?"

"It could have been either. Which do you think would be more likely?"

She shook her head and sipped from her glass. Then she put her glass down and turned to Nathan and shook her head again. "I don't know," she said. "It's—well, it's hard to imagine anybody who would—oh, go to that trouble. Any murderer. Of course, some women are hipped on modesty. Decency. Whatever you may call it. Not so many nowadays. But some, I guess. Only—"

She looked down at her glass, which was almost empty. She emptied it. She looked at his glass, which was still almost full. She raised eyebrows at him and lifted her shoulders. "All right," Nathan said. "I will in a minute. Only?"

"I'm thinking," Rose said, and put fresh ice in the shaker and measured a little gin and much less vermouth onto it, stirred and stirred and poured. This time she did not squeeze a sliver of lemon peel because she had brought only one from the kitchen, planning on her usual single drink. She did not immediately drink from her partly filled glass.

"Women don't really care about other women being—exposed. Naked, if it comes to that. Naked women aren't anything special to other women. Heterosexual women, I mean. I don't know much about the other kind. Of course—oh, I suppose there are some women who hate human bodies. Think them sinful. The woman you have in mind, Nathan? Because you have some woman in mind, haven't you?"

"As a possible," he said. "Oh, perhaps two. Mrs. Prentis is one of them. She—told me a strange thing today. Without being asked to."

He told her about Hope Prentis's self-imposed chastity.

"It's unbelievable," Rose said. "It's fanaticism."

"Yes."

"The poor man," Rose said. "Or—was he that way too?"

"I doubt it. He—a man gave him pictures of pretty girls. Who might guide him, accompany him, in his investigations of the city's vice. 'Guide' is the word that was used."

Rose Shapiro said, "My God!" and half emptied her half-filled glass. She said, "Are there really people like that? Like this Mrs. Prentis, I mean."

Nathan said, "Apparently," and drank from his own glass. He looked at it and drank again.

"Some kind of religious masochism? Or—didn't she care? Just frigid?"

"I don't know," Nathan said. "You think a woman is the more likely? About the clothes, I mean."

"I don't know," she said. "I—well, I don't think either is very likely. A woman—it doesn't seem to me that a woman would care very much. About how another woman—a dead woman—looked. I said that, didn't I? But about a woman like this Mrs. Prentis—" She raised her shoulders and let them drop again.

"A prudish man," she said then. "An—oh, an insanely prudish man. A fanatic about it. Is there a man like that, Nathan?"

"Yes," Nathan said, "there's a man who maybe's like that."

He set down his glass and went to the telephone.

He got the lieutenant on the four-to-midnight shift at Homicide South.

"Well," the lieutenant said, "Spencer's good with a camera. I don't know he looks much like the type goes around snapping people in restaurants. Or that the Wexley is the sort of place where that sort of thing's done much. But O.K. if you say so, Nate. He'll be dressed like a priest, you say?"

"If he's there at all. He may very well not be. It's just a chance."

"O.K.," Lieutenant O'Reilly said. "We'll have a shot at it, Nate. Spencer'll use a minicamera, but chances are, of course, he'll tumble to it."

"Yes," Shapiro said and his voice was sad almost to the point of hopelessness. "Chances are he will, Frank. I'd like the prints in the morning."

"Sure. If he gets the shots."

"If he gets the shots. And—there are boys down at Headquarters who can do a nice job of touching up."

"Yes, Nate. Thanks for telling me."

"Just getting straight in my own head, Frank. If he's wearing a clerical collar—backside to front—have them draw a necktie in. Or however they do it. Not on all the prints. On two or three, maybe."

"Four-in-hand? Or bow?"

"Four-in-hand. Dark, at a guess."

"You want them to change his clothes? Give him, maybe, a nice snappy sports jacket?"

"No," Shapiro said. "He's not a lily needs gilding, Frank. Decent black suit. He's a very decent man."

Francis X. O'Reilly said, "Spencer's on his way," and Nathan Shapiro went back to the sofa in front of the electric fire. He finished his drink and looked at the empty glass.

"You've opted for somebody," Rose said. "A priest, I take it."

"Ordained minister," Shapiro said. "He wouldn't call it priest. Papish, he'd call that, probably. Opted on the chance only, Rose. Because I haven't the faintest idea why he'd do it. Way it looks, he only stands to lose. No motive."

"You've told me," Rose said, "that it isn't necessary to prove a motive."

"Technically," Nathan said. "But juries like to know why. Come to that, so do detectives." He regarded his empty glass. Rose pulled it nearer and put ice cubes in it. He said, "I don't think I'd—"

"Medicinal," Rose said. "To ward off colds."

But this time she poured much less Scotch on the ice.

They had dinner. They sat in front of the fire and played records. A Brahms record and an Ella Fitzgerald record. A Beethoven and an Ethel Merman. "Share and share alike," Rose said, as he put the records on the changer. It was during the Beethoven that Nathan began to yawn.

"Go to bed," Rose said. "You're tired and sleepy. I'll clean things up and be along."

Nathan Shapiro said, "All right," in a sleepy voice and went into the bedroom. When she had rinsed dishes and put them in the washer she too went into the bedroom, and Nathan was in bed. Only, he was in her bed.

"You're supposed to be sleepy," she told him. "Very tired and sleepy."

"Not all that sleepy," Nathan said. "Of course, if I'm getting a cold—"

"Share and share alike," Rose Shapiro said, and slid out of clothes.

"Hello?"

"Police. Matter of routine. Can you account for your movements last night?"

"Home and in bed by ten. Asleep in ten minutes. Didn't stir all night."

"Doesn't jibe with what we hear. We hear you went to a movie. Eighth Street Playhouse."

"You've heard wrong, mister."

"It's supposed to be a good movie. Tomorrow, maybe. We can have dinner early somewhere and—"

"No, Tony. I'm getting a lamb stew from Bob the Butcher. We'll eat it here."

"Six-thirty?"

"Make it—oh, all right. Six-thirty. But this time we really go to the movie."

"Of course," Tony Cook said. "What else would we think of doing?"

"The movie," Rachel Farmer said. She spoke very firmly. But of course he was blocks away.

12

The photographs were pretty good, considering. For shots taken with what O'Reilly had called a "minicamera," they had blown up well. One showed the small, thin man sitting at a table in a restaurant—the coffee shop of the Hotel Wexley, but that didn't show. A second showed him, still at the table, from another angle. A third showed him walking out of the restaurant, toward the camera, and it was the best and most useful. If any of them was going to be useful.

There were two copies of each print. In one of each the Reverend John Wesley Higgs was wearing a clerical collar. It still looked too large for him; he seemed to peer out of it, as if he were peering over a wall. In the other prints he was wearing a plain white collar and a necktie. These retouched photographs were convincing enough if you didn't look at them too closely. Higgs was just a man in a dark suit, wearing a collar and a dark four-in-hand tie.

Shapiro put the photographs which showed the Reverend Mr. Higgs having dinner in the top drawer of his desk. He put the two versions of Higgs walking toward the camera, and apparently unaware of it, face down on top of his desk.

Shapiro read Tony Cook's report. There wasn't much doubt that Farmington had got kickbacks from the singers he had hired to hymn the praise of God. But there was a great deal of doubt whether it could be proved. They could, Tony thought, get plenty of the men and women to say they had paid. But he had found none who could testify it was pay if you want the job. And all had put their money envelopes in a box marked with the name of the Mission of Redemption, Inc. and had been told they were making voluntary contributions to a sacred cause. And suppose Farmington had taken the envelopes out of the box and put them in a briefcase? You don't leave money lying around loose.

It would be difficult to prove that Farmington had kept the money. Probably it would be impossible. And it was not, at least directly, within the province of Homicide South.

It was a little after nine when Shapiro got to writing his own report—the report, he thought, he should have written yesterday. Not that there was anything especially urgent in it. Mr. and Mrs. Jonathan Prentis had not, for eight of their ten years of marriage, had sexual intercourse because, if there is no expectation of children, intercourse is a sin. Mrs. Prentis had spent five or six days in a rather bleak retreat near North White Plains. (Detective Lieutenant Nathan Shapiro had got his feet wet. But he had not caught cold. Yet, anyway.)

It was taking a time to round them up, Shapiro thought, at a quarter of ten. But he had supposed it would. They would have had to be waked up, as well as rounded up. The big-eyed bus boy would be frightened again. Nobody would be happy.

It was a little after ten when Tony Cook came to say they were all on hand—Manuel Perez with the large frightened eyes; André Brideaux, Emile Schmidt and Granzo (who probably would be indignant) and the doorman, who was named Rex Prince. And whom they had missed the first time around because they had not known the Village Brawl ran to a doorman. And had not thought to ask. Which proves, if it needs proving, that I'm not much good at the job and that the department is stupid not to know it.

"Bring them in one at a time," Shapiro told Tony Cook. "Start with the kid, because he's scared of the fuzz. We may as well let him get it over with."

Manuel Perez was wearing a black leather jacket and, below tight slacks, black shoes with straps on them. He looked scared; there was fear in his large dark eyes. As soon as Tony Cook brought him into the room, walking behind him and towering over him, Manuel said, "Sir. I didn't do bad thing, sir." And then he went into Spanish, talking very rapidly and excitedly. Shapiro didn't understand the hurried Spanish.

"All right, son," Nathan Shapiro said. "Nobody thinks you

did anything bad. Just maybe that you can help us. Come over here, son."

It was only a few steps in the small office from door to desk. Manuel Perez took them hesitantly. After the first he turned back to look at the door, but Tony Cook was standing in front of it. The boy went on, as if into a trap. "It's all right, son," Shapiro said. "Nobody's going to hurt you. Look at this."

Shapiro put one of the photographs where Manuel could look down at it. It was one of the Reverend Higgs wearing a clerical collar. Shapiro said, "Ever see him anywhere, son?"

"He's a priest," Manuel said. "Isn't he a priest, sir?"

"Dressed like one, anyway," Shapiro said. "Ever see him, Manuel?"

"No, sir, I don't think so. I go to mass; sir. Every Sunday I go to mass."

"That's fine," Shapiro said. "You don't know this man?"

"No, sir."

"This one?" Shapiro said, and showed him the photograph which had been worked over so that Higgs appeared dressed in a dark business suit, with a dark necktie.

Manuel Perez looked at it. He looked longer than he had at the other. Then he looked at Shapiro. He said, "But it's the same man as the other, sir? Isn't it, sir? Only not a priest."

"You've got good eyes, son," Shapiro told him. "You ever see this man dressed this way?"

"I don't think so, sir. Only maybe I did but don't remember. I try to remember, sir. Not the priest, sir. Maybe this one, but I don't know. In the restaurant there are lots of people, sir, and I run run run. Would he have be—I mean been—in the restaurant?"

"I don't know," Shapiro said. "We're trying to find out, son. You never saw him there, Manuel? Dressed as a priest or not?"

"Priests don't come there, sir. I never saw a priest there."

"All right, son," Shapiro said. "Want to see he gets a ride back home, Tony?"

"Sure," Tony Cook said, "I'll see—"

"Please, sirs," Manuel said. "Please. Not in a police car. Not down where I live. They'd think I—I don't know, sirs. It would be bad for me. They'd think I—" He did not finish, at least in English. But he spoke rapidly, excitedly, in Spanish.

"All right," Shapiro said. "They'd think you'd sold out to the fuzz. Something like that. Go home any way you like, Manuel. See that he gets out all right, Tony. And ask Mr. Schmidt to come in."

Manuel Perez did not run across the office to the door. But he moved very rapidly to the door, and Tony Cook opened it for him and went out after him. Probably, Shapiro thought, the kid had expected to be beaten up. We're the enemy, Shapiro thought. It's too damn bad, but that's the way it is.

Emile Schmidt looked just as German as ever in a tweed jacket and gray slacks and a very wide necktie. He was not at all afraid. He looked at both photographs and shook his head. He said, "Not that I remember, Lieutenant. Would it have been at the restaurant?"

"It might have been," Shapiro said.

"Priests don't come there," Emile said. "They like quieter places. I worked over at Charles for a while a couple of years back. Priests used to come in there sometimes. But that was before they dolled the place up. I don't know about now."

"But this man. You don't remember ever seeing him?"

"I'm afraid I don't, sir."

"If you don't you don't," Shapiro said. "Sorry to have waked you up, Mr. Schmidt."

Schmidt went out of the office. He didn't hurry to the door. He did walk a little as if his feet hurt. But after all he was a waiter. Probably his feet hurt most of the time.

"Priests do go to Charles," Tony said. "Did in the old days. Food's good there, and they like to go where the food's good. Like they say about truck drivers."

Shapiro was thinking, disconsolately, that, as usual, he wasn't getting anywhere. Then he heard Tony's last sentence and looked up at him and shook his head.

"Eating places along highways," Tony said. "If truck drivers stop at them, the food's good, people keep saying. Which is a lot of baloney, actually. They stop where there's room to park their rigs. Who next, Nate?"

"Granzo, I think," Shapiro said, and Tony went to get Granzo. He came back with him. Granzo was very neat in a blue suit which was fitted in at the waist. He looked sleepy.

He had never seen the man in either photograph. At least, he didn't remember ever seeing him.

"Thing is," Granzo said. "He looks like you could see him and not see him. Know what I mean?"

"Yes," Shapiro said.

"If he had that collar on, like a priest's collar," Granzo said, "and came in to the Brawl I'd remember him. Because priests don't. Anyway, I wouldn't want them to, know what I mean? Because they'd make some people feel they oughtn't to have a good time."

"But you don't remember him dressed either way? Last Wednesday night? Thursday morning? At the restaurant?"

"No. Was he there, you think? He could have been, maybe, because we had a rush. With this—this man got killed?"

"We don't know," Shapiro said. "We're trying to find out. Anyway, you don't remember him?"

"No. How tall is he?"

"Not tall. Five six. Maybe only five five."

Granzo looked for a moment like a man in thought. But then he shook his head.

"All right," Shapiro said. "Sorry we had to wake you up, Mr. Granzo."

"All the time people wake me up," Granzo said. "So I get waked up."

"André Brideaux," Shapiro said, when Granzo had gone. Tony got Brideaux.

Brideaux wore a sports jacket with a good deal of green in it and dark slacks and a sports shirt which was all green. And he looked at both pictures carefully and shook his head over both. He said, "Same man, isn't it, m'sieu?" He was told it was the same man. "No, m'sieu, I guess not," and then, "He a tall man?"

"About your height," Shapiro said.

"Seems like I saw a man dressed that way," Brideaux said. "Ordinary collar, though. Standing just inside the door and looking around, the way they do sometimes. Wondering if it's going to cost too much. Sometimes they just look around and go out. Sometimes a man and a woman come in together and look the place over and decide it looks too rich for their blood. Or's too noisy or something. Sometimes I figure the man comes in alone first and sometimes the woman does."

"Wednesday night," Shapiro said. "Could it have been Wednesday night you saw a man dressed the way this man is? Dark suit? Dark tie? Man about five feet six?"

"M'sieu," André said, "I know what night you mean. The night this guy got killed. Been jammed up ever since. People are morbid, sort of."

"Yes," Shapiro said. "The man you saw. He may have been this man?"

"Could be. Could not be. That's all I can tell you, m'sieu. Maybe yes. Maybe no."

"Stood inside the door and looked around," Shapiro said. "Come in and get a table? Or go out, the way you say some of them do?"

"M'sieu, I was working. We were busy. I don't know what he did."

"Before or after you seated Mr. Prentis?"

Brideaux shook his head hopelessly.

"Before or after the girl joined Mr. Prentis in the booth?"

Brideaux shook his head again. He said, "M'sieu, I told you I couldn't say it was this man. Just a not very tall man, like me, in a dark suit. Could have been anybody. Town's full of men like that."

"Yes," Shapiro said. "Thanks for coming in, Mr. Brideaux. Sorry to have waked you up. Brought you all the way down here."

"It's O.K.," Brideaux said. "Anyway, I guess you had to."

"We're not getting much of anywhere, are we?" Tony Cook said after Brideaux had gone out of the office.

Shapiro's face drooped. He shook his head. He said, "The doorman. What's his name, Tony?"

"Believe it or not, he says it's Rex Prince."

"I'll try to believe it," Shapiro said. "Bring him in, Tony."

The doorman was as tall as Tony Cook and almost as broad of shoulder. He was young. He had a pleasant, squarish face.

Shapiro said, "Mr. Prince?" and the man smiled and said, "Rex Prince, sir. You can blame my parents."

There seemed to be no answer to that except an agreeing smile and a nod of the head. Shapiro provided both. He opened the top drawer of his desk and took out a photograph of Janet Rushton and put it where Prince could see it. He said, "Remember ever seeing this girl, Mr. Prince?"

Prince picked the photograph up and looked at it and said, "She's good-looking, isn't she? Looks kind of familiar. An actress, or something?"

"She was a singer," Shapiro said, and Prince looked down at him and said, "Was, Lieutenant?"

"Yes," Shapiro said. "She's dead, Mr. Prince."

"Pity," Prince said. "Good-looking girl. Never sang at the Brawl that I know of."

"No," Shapiro said. "I don't know that she ever did. But—you connect her with the restaurant?"

Prince shrugged his broad shoulders. He said, "Sort of, maybe. Could be she's in one of my classes, but that doesn't seem right. Maybe I just went some place she was singing."

"Classes?" Shapiro said.

"N.Y.U.," Prince said. "I go there daytimes. Nights I get people taxis. Pretty sure it isn't at the university I saw her. If I ever did see her. If she's not—if she wasn't—just a pretty girl like—" He stopped abruptly. He said, "Wait a minute."

Shapiro waited less than a minute.

"Taxi," Prince said. "That's it. I got her a taxi and she gave me a dollar. Usually it's a quarter. Sometimes with women just a dime. Couple or three nights ago, I think it was."

"At the restaurant?"

"Sure. Hey, it was the night this man got killed. That's the night it was."

"Tell me about it, Mr. Prince," Shapiro said. "I suppose she came out of the restaurant and—"

She had come out of the restaurant and come out alone. Prince couldn't be sure about the time. Perhaps it had been one-thirty or thereabouts. It had, he was certain, been before the time people began to crowd out of the Village Brawl, as they did after two, when the band stopped playing.

It was unusual for a woman to come out alone, but it was not unprecedented.

"Sometimes they have quarrels with the guys they're with. Sometimes, I guess the guys get drunk. So they walk out."

Usually they got taxis; if they were in their right mind they got taxis. "Women don't walk around here much at night if they've got sense. Not alone they don't. It isn't safe."

"All right," Shapiro said. "I know it isn't safe. This girl—you're pretty sure it was this girl?"

"Now I am. Because now I remember she gave me a dollar."

"Came out alone and asked you to get her a taxi?"

"I said, 'Get you a taxi, miss?' and she said, 'Please.' So I went out and flagged one down. I was lucky. Of course, a lot of the hackers keep an eye on the Brawl about that time of night. So the cab pulled up and—"

"Wait a minute, Mr. Prince," Shapiro said.

He got the photographs of Higgs out of the desk drawer and put the one with the simulated necktie on top and pushed the glossies on the desk so Prince could see them. Shapiro said, "Ever see this man that you remember?"

"Looks pretty much like just anybody, doesn't it?"

"Yes," Shapiro said. "I suppose he does. Only—"

"Wait a minute," Prince said. "Sort of a short man?"

"Yes. Anyway, not tall."

"Man like that," Prince said. "I don't say that man, but he had on a dark suit and wasn't very tall. Man like that's as far as I can go."

"Yes?"

"When I'd got the cab and opened the door and turned back to say, 'All right, miss,' she wasn't looking at me or the cab. She was looking down the street at a man who was coming along toward us. The way you look at somebody you think maybe you know, or ought to know, but aren't sure about. You know how it is, Lieutenant?"

Shapiro said he knew how it was.

"First," Prince said, "I thought he was a friend of hers and she was going to say, 'Hello,' or something. 'Hi, there,' or something. She—oh, sort of hesitated."

"But she didn't say anything?"

"No. He was pretty close by then and he just kept walking along. Looking—oh, looking through her. As if he'd never seen her before. So—well, I thought she sort of shrugged her shoulders, as if she'd made a mistake. And I guess she had."

"It was light? Light enough to see by?"

"Sure. Plenty of light."

"Then?"

"Then she opened her handbag and began to grope around in it, the way they do looking for change. But she couldn't find any—looked in a coin purse, way I remember it—and then got out a billfold and took a dollar bill out of it and gave me that. I said, 'Thank you, miss,' and held the cab door open for her and closed it after she'd got in."

"Did you hear where she told the driver to take her?"

"No. It wasn't any of my business."

"The man she apparently thought she knew and decided she didn't know. He just walk on up the street?"

"I don't know. I wasn't paying any attention to him. Anyway, a couple came out of the restaurant and wanted a cab, and I went out in the street and blew the whistle and waved. Took longer that time, as I remember it. Sometimes there'll be two or three in a bunch with the top lights on and sometimes it'll take five-ten minutes."

"This man you saw. Who might have been this man." Shapiro tapped the photograph with his fingers. "He could have gone into the restaurant?"

"Could have, I guess. I can't say he did and I can't say he didn't. I'm sorry, Lieutenant."

"No reason you should be," Shapiro told him. "You saw quite a bit, Mr. Prince."

"Remember," Prince said, "I can't swear it was this girl, Lieutenant. Much less this man. I just think it was maybe this girl. Could have been. Because not very many people tip a dollar just to get a cab. Not if they're sober, and this girl was. That all, Lieutenant?"

"I guess that's—" Shapiro said and stopped. "No," he said. "I want you to do something else, Mr. Prince. Go back and sit where you were sitting before you came in here. Oh, for an hour or so. There'll be people walking past you. Coming here or going to one of the other offices. I'd like you just to look at them. If you see anybody you've seen before, or think maybe you've seen before, tell Detective Cook here. Or signal him. He'll be at his desk. He'll keep an eye on you."

"Well," Prince said, "thing is, Lieutenant, I've got an eleven-o'clock class. Math, and I'm finding math rather tough going. But—"

"Yes, Mr. Prince," Shapiro said. "I'm going to ask you to cut the class. Because the way people walk is often identifying."

"This man?" Prince said and pointed to the photograph.

"Anybody who looks familiar."

"This girl. This good-looking girl. Did somebody kill her, Lieutenant?"

"Yes, Mr. Prince. Somebody killed her."

"O.K.," Prince said. "For that I'll cut the class. Because she was a good-looking girl and—well, it's a hell of a waste."

Shapiro said, "Thanks, Mr. Prince. It may be an hour or so," and felt oddly reassured, as one does when returning to a normal world from a world of fantasy.

Prince went out with Tony Cook to sit in a chair from which he could see those who walked along a corridor from the squad room toward the offices, one of which was Shapiro's and one that of Captain William Weigand, commanding, and toward the interrogation rooms beyond.

Tony Cook would see that men walked along it, so that Rex Prince would have a choice. The chances were high that if he made one it would be the wrong one. He'd pick Detective (2nd gr.) Timothy Maxwell. Or somebody off the street come in with a squeal. Identifications are flimsy things, and Prince had seen the man Janet Rushton appeared to know only briefly, and the light had not been all that good. But the whole thing was flimsy. It was as much hunch as anything else.

Nathan Shapiro sighed and shook a frustrated head and went to Weigand's office. The door was partly opened, and Bill Weigand was talking on the telephone. He was saying, "I know, Andy. Nobody ever hears anything. Or thinks it was a backfire. Right? But just keep asking."

He listened a minute. He said, "Right. Keep on looking in ash cans."

He put the telephone in its cradle and said, "Andy's a good man, but he does want his hand held."

"So do I," Shapiro told him and sat on a wooden chair. "And approval. But it'll be a shot in the dark. It may bounce back."

"They do sometimes," Bill Weigand said. "But go ahead, Nate."

Nathan Shapiro went ahead. When he had finished, Weigand said, "It is pretty thin. Even if you get an identification—a halfway identification—it will be thin, Nate."

Shapiro nodded his head in agreement.

"And the question is, why, Nate? Everybody stands to lose because the whole enterprise falls apart and everybody—well, spills out. And juries like motives. We both know that. Good, substantial motives. Like standing to gain a million dollars. Or, hell, two dollars and fifty cents."

"Yes," Shapiro said. "We both know that, Bill."

"On what you've got—which is damn near nothing; which is nothing but a guess—the D.A.'s office won't go along. Because they don't like to go along to nowhere."

Nathan said that he knew, and his voice was dispirited.

"They'll want to sit in," Weigand said. "They've got to approve."

Shapiro didn't say anything to that, because Bill Weigand was talking to himself, repeating what they both knew—the Homicide Bureau of the District Attorney's office has to approve a homicide charge and doesn't like to unless it's pretty sure it can be made to stick.

"Here?" Weigand said.

"Yes. With the recorder running. And nobody has to say anything and is entitled to be represented by counsel. So anybody in his right mind clams up. Only—"

He let it hang there and Bill Weigand waited for some seconds and then said, "You think he isn't, Nate?"

"I don't know, Bill. They're—they're all strange to me. I told you at the start they would be. That I was the wrong—"

"Yes," Bill Weigand said. "Trouble is, you always say that, Nate. And it turns out not to be true. All right. These people are a long way from your world. From mine, too, come to that.

As far from mine as from yours, although now and then I go to church the way you, now and then, go to the temple. That doesn't enter, Nate. They're—hell, they're people—right?"

"I guess so," Nathan said, the doubt still in his voice. "Oh, sure. Fanatics are people."

"You've got a hunch about the why, Nate?"

Nathan hesitated for some time—for a long enough time to get a cigarette out and get it lighted. But then, slowly, he nodded his head.

"Yes," he said. "It's preposterous, but I maybe have."

Weigand waited but Nathan Shapiro only shook his head again.

"Right," Bill Weigand said, "have him brought down. And I'll get onto the D.A.'s office. Bernie Simmons will see somebody's sent along to sit in. Take half an hour or so, probably."

"Take that long to get him down here, probably," Shapiro said and went back to his office and his telephone. He called the uptown precinct and got Captain Maloney and told him what was wanted. He said, "Not together. The man first. And Detective Flanders with the woman. O.K.?"

"You're free with precinct cars," Maloney said. "But O.K., Nate."

Shapiro sat at his desk with the office door partly open so that he could see who walked up and down the corridor. Quite a few did.

13

After about half an hour, during which Nathan Shapiro had ample time to assure himself that he was, as usual, making one hell of a mistake, a youngish man in a dark suit which included a vest walked past the open door. He had smooth black hair, neatly cut, and Shapiro flicked fingers along the back of his own neck. Yes, he needed a haircut. Rose should have reminded him.

The black-haired youngish man's footfalls stopped after a second or two, and Shapiro knew he had gone into Weigand's office, the right number of steps up the corridor. Then he heard the footsteps coming back. O.K. The man had looked like a lawyer. One of the new ones, probably. They changed around a lot.

The man came into the office, and Shapiro stood up behind his desk.

"Ogden. D.A.'s office," the man with black hair said. "The captain says you're the one to see. That if it's cracked, you've cracked it."

He held out a sleek hand, and Shapiro reached across the desk and shook it. It was a fine, firm handshake with no nonsense about it. Not, Shapiro thought, a man to be sympathetic about a shot in the dark; about a wild guess. And not a man likely to have met many people like those connected with the Mission of Redemption, Inc. Episcopalian, at a guess. High Church, probably.

"I'm not sure it's cracked," Shapiro said. "Sit down, Mr. Ogden, and I'll fill you in."

He rather expected Ogden to dust off the chair before he sat on it. Ogden didn't. He did reach back to close the office door and Shapiro said, "Rather you didn't, Mr. Ogden," and Ogden raised black eyebrows and shrugged square shoulders and sat down, with, Shapiro thought, the aspect of a man who will listen to anything, however preposterous.

He listened for about ten minutes while Shapiro filled him in. The expression on Ogden's face did nothing to add to Nathan Shapiro's confidence.

"It isn't much, is it?" Ogden said. "We can't get an indictment on what you've got. Let alone a conviction. You know how the boss feels about things like that, don't you, Lieutenant?"

"Yes," Shapiro said. "I know how he feels about it. We may get more."

Ogden said, "Mmmm." He said, "They do sound like a screwy bunch. But not screwy enough to give us anything on a platter. You think this doorman will recognize him?"

"I don't know."

"There was light enough?"

"The street's well lighted. There's a tube of light around the entrance. Prince thinks there was light enough. Except—he wasn't looking at the man. He was looking at the girl."

"Funny sort of name, Prince's," Ogden said. "Rex Prince rather lays it on, doesn't it?" But then he smiled, and the smile changed his face. "Come to that," he said, "Cornelius Ogden the Third rather lays it on too. You can guess what it boils down to, can't you?"

"Neal, probably."

"No," Ogden said. "Corny. Something to live down. They're on their way—"

He did not finish because Shapiro was looking beyond him, through the open door. Ogden turned to look that way too, but he was too late to see Mrs. Jonathan Prentis going along the hall with Detective Grace Flanders's hand firmly on the blonde woman's elbow. Mrs. Prentis had been looking straight ahead when he saw her. She had, he thought, been walking rather mechanically. She had been dressed in black, and loosely dressed so that curves were hidden.

"Mrs. Prentis," Shapiro said. "We'll give it about fifteen minutes. O.K.?"

"Well," Ogden said, "I can't say I get it, Lieutenant. But it's your party." He took a pack of cigarettes out of his pocket and shook cigarettes loose in it and held it across the desk to Shapiro. Shapiro took a cigarette and was reaching in his pocket for a lighter when Ogden held a light out to him—a light which leaped from a lighter which looked like being silver.

Ogden lighted his own cigarette. He said, "We just sit here and twiddle our thumbs."

"For now," Shapiro said. "And hope that the Reverend Mr. Higgs is twiddling his."

Ogden grinned, which changed his regular face even more than the smile had.

"Psychology," he said. "In the absence of anything more tangible."

Shapiro admitted it came to that. He got up and closed the office door.

"Simmons thinks you're good," Ogden said. "Bernard Simmons. He's my boss. I just got switched to Homicide. Bernie Simmons is quite a guy."

That seemed, for the moment, to exhaust the subject of Bernard Simmons, deputy chief of the District Attorney's Homicide Bureau. Shapiro went back to taking papers from the In basket and reading them and putting initials on them and, for the most part, putting them in the Out basket. Cornelius Ogden III finished his cigarette and stubbed it out, being careful that it would not be left to smolder. He went across the small office and looked out its single window. Shapiro knew what he would see from it—a bleak-looking building and, at the bottom, a cement paving with, probably, newspapers blowing around on it. It was a view which always depressed Nathan Shapiro.

It was twenty minutes before there was a *tat-tat-tat* on the door. Shapiro said, "Yes, Tony," and Tony Cook came in. Ogden turned from the window, and Shapiro said, "Mr. Ogden, Tony. From the D.A.'s office," and "Detective Anthony Cook, Mr. Ogden." Then he looked at Tony Cook and waited.

"Maybe yes, maybe no," Tony said. "A little inclined to yes from the way he walks. But nothing he can swear to."

"All right," Shapiro said. "All we had to expect. Mrs. Prentis and Mr. Higgs?"

"She didn't see him, as far as she showed. Didn't appear to look that way. He—yes, he saw her. Started to get up from his chair and didn't."

"Look any particular way? Surprised? Upset?"

Tony shrugged his shoulders and then shook his head. He said, "It isn't a face tells you much, Lieutenant. Just stays a face."

Shapiro stood up and came around the desk.

"May as well come along, Tony," Shapiro said.

Tony said, "Prince?"

"He's already missed his class," Shapiro said. "Mr. Higgs will be going back that way. Prince may as well have another look."

He led the way down the corridor to the one of the interrogation rooms Mrs. Prentis was not waiting in. He unlocked the door and they went into a large room, not harshly lighted, with an oblong table and several wooden chairs. Higgs was sitting in one of the chairs. Ogden and Nathan Shapiro and Cook sat in chairs across the table. Higgs looked from one to the other. He said, "I do not understand this, Lieutenant Shapiro. I have much to do. I was in the middle of an article. We have decided to continue those, at least for the time being."

"We'll try not to keep you too long, Mr. Higgs," Shapiro said. "One or two little points. This is Mr. Ogden, by the way. From the District Attorney's office."

Higgs looked at Ogden and nodded his head.

Higgs wore a clerical collar which was still a little too large for him. His eyes were still set rather closely together. His voice still grated.

"One point is about Mrs. Prentis," Shapiro said. "Late last month, we've learned, she came east. Went into a retreat near White Plains. You knew about that, Mr. Higgs?"

"Yes. I knew about that. It is a place for meditation and prayer. I have myself sought refuge there from time to time."

"Did Mrs. Prentis often go to this retreat? Or others like it?"

"Before the meetings," Higgs said. "I believe she often went to—to prepare herself. To commune with the Holy Spirit. While the Voice was seeking out the sins of a city."

Ogden looked at Shapiro and raised his eyebrows.

"Her husband," Shapiro said. "The Reverend Mr. Jonathan

Prentis. They called him 'the Voice.' 'The voice of one crying in the wilderness.' And also because, they tell me, he had a rather remarkable voice of his own. Speaking voice."

Ogden said, "Oh," and nodded his well-groomed head.

"Actually, Mr. Higgs," Shapiro said, "you went up to this retreat twice while she was there. To visit her. Is that right?"

"Yes. That is right, Lieutenant. But I don't see what—"

"Why did you go, Mr. Higgs?"

"To join my prayers with hers. To find sustenance in her abiding faith. She is a saintly woman, Lieutenant. She holds up our hands."

Ogden looked somewhat bewildered. Not like anything he's heard before, Shapiro thought. Any more than I had.

"Just to join her in prayer," Shapiro said to the Reverend Higgs. "Nothing more than that, Mr. Higgs?"

"There can be no more than that," Higgs said. "Surely that is true in your faith also, Lieutenant."

"Yes," Shapiro said, with no inflection on the word. "Mr. Higgs, when you went up to see Mrs. Prentis. It wasn't to tell her what her husband was up to?"

"Up to?"

"In his—research," Shapiro said, and made the pause evident. "In this research of his, he was being guided—that's the word Mr. Farmington uses—by a very attractive young woman. One who, let's say, knew her way around."

"Did Farmington tell you that?"

"Yes. He—well, more or less supplied Mr. Prentis with such guides. From among the young women he hired to sing in the choir. You knew about that, didn't you, Mr. Higgs?"

Higgs's eyes seemed to draw closer together. But, of course, one imagines things about other faces.

"If you are implying—" Higgs said and stopped and swallowed inside the large white collar. "The Reverend Prentis was a man of God, Lieutenant."

"I'm implying," Shapiro said, "that Mr. Prentis was playing around. Or that you thought he was. With a girl named Janet Rushton. You did know that, didn't you?"

"I—well, Mr. Farmington hinted at something like that. I

did not believe him. Because the Reverend Prentis was a dedicated man. A man of—"

"Yes," Shapiro said. "You've told us that before. Did you tell Mrs. Prentis what her husband was up to?"

Ogden tapped his fingers lightly on the table.

"Yes," Shapiro said. "You don't have to answer that, Mr. Higgs. You don't have to answer anything unless you choose to. You are entitled to have counsel present to advise you of your rights. And what we are saying in this room is being recorded. Enough, Mr. Ogden?"

"Yes," Ogden said. "Do you want to call a lawyer, Mr. Higgs. To advise you?"

"There is no need," Higgs said. "I put my trust in God. He is my adviser."

"As you want it," Shapiro said. "When you visited Mrs. Prentis at the retreat, did you tell her about her husband? Perhaps the first time what you only suspected. What Farmington had told you. Or hinted to you. Perhaps on the second visit that you had—had verified?"

Higgs said, "Well," drawing it out. He looked from one to the other of the men facing him across the table. He said, "Well," again. Then he said, "Did she tell you that? Today? After you brought her down here?"

"I take it, Mr. Higgs, you saw her come in?"

"Yes. As if—as if she were being arrested."

"Nobody's being arrested," Shapiro said, and, again after a pause, added, "yet."

"And she told you," Higgs said, saving Shapiro the lie he had been entirely prepared to tell. "All right. She was his wife. They were linked in the bonds of holy matrimony. She had a right to know."

"One way of looking at it," Shapiro said. "How did she take it, Mr. Higgs? Very upset?"

"With disbelief," Higgs said. "As I had when Mr. Farmington first hinted that—first hinted about it. That he should turn from God. Betray the Lord he served. At first it was impossible to believe. For her as it was for me."

"But, on the second visit, you convinced her?"

"Yes. She said, 'No! No! It cannot be.' But I am sure she was convinced."

"And then?"

Higgs did not know what he meant.

"She said, 'No. No.' And then? Was she angry? Because he had proved unfaithful. To her as to his—vocation?"

"She was—she seemed broken."

"And angry? In what people call a jealous rage? Because, Mr. Higgs, in that kind of anger people have killed."

"There is no violence in Hope Prentis. She is a saintly woman. Anyway, she was ill that night. And asleep in her room. Mrs. Mathews has told you that."

"She could have pretended sleep. Followed her husband when he went out. With an ice pick in her handbag."

Unexpectedly, Higgs doubled his hands into fists and rapped on the table with the knuckles of his fists.

"No," he said. "That is impossible. I—she would have been seen."

Tony and Ogden both looked quickly at Shapiro, but Shapiro looked only at John Wesley Higgs.

"Probably," Shapiro said. "When you convinced Mrs. Prentis of her husband's infidelity. How did you do that?"

"I had—I had proved it to myself."

"How?"

"I—I saw them meeting. Several times. Going to places of iniquity. Where liquor is served and dancing is allowed. And, twice, I saw him go into this house she lived in. Late at night. After she had gone in. To join her."

"I take it you followed them, Mr. Higgs. Or him from his hotel downtown. That right? Followed them several times, apparently. To get proof to pass on to Mrs. Prentis?"

"It was my duty, Lieutenant. It was a task laid on me by the Almighty. That came to me in prayer. You would not understand."

"Perhaps not," Shapiro said. "The Almighty laid an—er—injunction on you? To follow Prentis and the girl. You know the girl is dead, don't you? The girl named Janet Rushton? The girl, I suppose, you saw him with?"

"Yes," Higgs said. "The wages of sin is death. They had sinned together."

"And both are dead," Shapiro said. "Wednesday night. After the meeting. You followed Prentis when he left the hotel uptown. A minute ago you started to say you would have seen Mrs. Prentis if she had followed her husband. You caught yourself. But that was what you started to say, wasn't it?"

"He had spoken the words of God. The words God put into my mind to write for him. He had brought hundreds to redemption. He went out to sin again."

"And you followed?"

"I was the instrument of God. I followed as He ordained. I was chosen for the task. I, not another. It was I—I—the Lord chose to do His work."

"Followed to this restaurant in the Village," Shapiro said. "Saw him go in. And waited? Until Miss Rushton came. Alone, I take it?"

"In a taxi. Yes. They—it was a way they had behaved before. In the places they went, the forces of evil would conspire with them. Would deny that they had been together. Drinking liquor. Laughing."

The inflection in his harsh voice made laughter sinful.

"They were together that night?" Shapiro said. "When you went into the restaurant and stood near the door until you saw them together?"

"The people there were wanton," Higgs said. "Dancing to worldly music. Drinking liquor. Yes, I saw them. A waiter brought them glasses. They drank together."

"You saw them together in the restaurant. Then what did you do?"

"What God laid upon me. I was His instrument. His avenging sword."

His harsh voice went up until he was almost shouting across the long, narrow table.

Shapiro's voice, by contrast, was low. It was almost a gentle voice.

"You went outside and waited, out of sight, until she came out," Shapiro said. "Only you moved too quickly, didn't you?

Came out of the shadows you had been hiding in before she had got into the cab. So that she saw you. Knew who you were. And—saw you go into the restaurant?"

"To avenge his sin against the Lord. It was laid upon me. On *me*. I was the chosen one. His eyes had been upon me as I served Him. Humbled myself and served Him. So it was I who was chosen. I was the elect. I—"

His voice faded out. He put his hands flat on the table and leaned forward a little and stared at the sad-faced man across from him.

"Carrying the ice pick," Shapiro said. "That you'd brought with you from the hotel? Or, picked up at a hardware store nearby?"

"The day before," Higgs said. "When I knew I had been chosen as God's instrument. To bring His vengeance on this sinful man."

"Came up behind him," Shapiro said, "and killed him with the ice pick. Did he see you? Before he died?"

"He had just finished drinking and put his glass down. He was leaning forward to get his wallet out of a hip pocket. He did not see me."

"But the girl had. Recognized you. So you went to her apartment, where you had seen them go, and killed her too. Did she let you in, Higgs?"

"The doors were unlocked," Higgs said. "She had left them so for him. So that they might sin together."

"Smothered her," Shapiro said. "Then smoothed her dress down. Very carefully so as to cover her. Why, Mr. Higgs?"

"There is," John Wesley Higgs said, "such a thing as decency."

"He really said that?" Rachel Farmer said. "After he had killed two people he said there is such a thing as decency? He must—he must be crazy."

They were in the Gay Street apartment. Their glasses had been filled and clicked together. In the kitchen a lamb stew, concocted by Bob the Butcher, was heating in a double boiler. Tonight they were going to the movie. Tonight they were really going to the movie.

"A religious fanatic," Tony Cook said. "Whether—well, whether it comes to the same thing will be up to the psychiatrists. Ogden thinks they'll find him fit to stand trial. His lawyer—provided he finally decides to employ a mortal one—will contend he's legally insane. His statement—the one he finally signed—is pretty rambling. Full of tag ends from the Bible. Not a very coherent document. But a confession."

"And," Rachel said, "all you have. It's—it's still crazy, Tony. An instrument of the Almighty. Delegated to avenge sin."

"Not quite all we have," Tony said. "When we took him out, Prince was pretty positive. He was walking toward Prince, as he had that night. Prince is pretty sure from the way he walks."

"Didn't Mr. Higgs ever go to Sunday school, Tony?" Rachel said.

Tony looked at her blankly. He put his glass down on the table in front of them so he could concentrate. Finally he merely shook a puzzled head.

"Because," Rachel said, "I did. And I remember tag ends. And somewhere in the Bible it says, 'Vengeance is mine; I will repay, saith the Lord.' And he must believe eveything that's in the Bible. Was it just that? I mean—to root out sin and destroy the sinners? However it was in his crazy mind?"

"I don't know," Tony Cook said, and picked up his glass again. "I'm not much good at seeing into other people's minds. And Nate thinks he isn't, but—"

He sipped from his glass. He shook his head again.

"It's hard to tell about Nate," he said. "He has this thing about not understanding people. But when we talked it over, after Higgs had been booked, he said that being second fiddle all his life can do strange things to a man. Higgs wrote Prentis's sermons and syndicate articles. He makes a point of that, now. But the credit—before the audiences and I guess Higgs thought before God—went to Prentis. Because Prentis was tall and good-looking and had this amazing voice. The voice we heard. And, all through his final statement, Higgs keeps saying over and over that *he* was the one chosen—he. Not anybody else. '*I* was the instrument of the Lord. *I* was the chosen one.' To get it down to the way people talk, 'I was the big shot.' For the first time in his life, Nate thinks. I don't know. But when

Nate pretended to suspect Mrs. Prentis, it—well, it shook out of Higgs."

"The star," Rachel said. "Not the understudy any more. Is that what Lieutenant Shapiro thinks? And—what he thought would happen? That Higgs would—oh, claim the leading role?"

"Yes," Tony said. "The way Nate had worked it out."

"It's all sort of—oh, dreadful, isn't it? Weird and dreadful. Because a man and a woman—were they really sleeping together?"

"We don't know," Tony said. "Nobody'll ever know. I suppose so. His wife held out on him. Because sex is—"

"I know," Rachel said. "A carnal sin unless children come of it."

She emptied her sherry glass. She held it out.

"Tony," she said, "let's have another drink and some lamb stew and go to the movie. It's for mature audiences only and a lot of the time they won't be wearing many clothes. But, compared to some things, it'll be decent, Tony. And there's such a thing as decency."

Suddenly she shivered, so that the glass she held out trembled in her hand.

He took it from her and carried it, and his own, to the table they used for a bar. He filled both glasses.

Tonight, he thought, we really will to go the movie. To take a bad taste out of our mouths.